The Lion Tamer's Daughter

Written by Alyssa Helton

Copyright © 2016 Alyssa Helton

ISBN-13: 978-1539882176
ISBN-10: 1539882179

Character illustrations by Stephen Martin
Cover design by Lisabook on Fiverr

Dedication

This book is dedicated to my best friend, my husband Keith. Without you, I would never have reached for these goals, let alone achieve them. Love you, babe.

PROLOGUE

I approached the old home with its weathered siding yellowed by dirt and sunlight, and knocked on the rusty screen door. The door rattled and alerted a small dog inside who considered it his duty to bark incessantly until his owner hushed him with a swat from a rolled newspaper. A middle-aged man opened the door and looked me over head to toe before uttering a word.

"Can I help you?" he demanded.

"Yes, Sir. I'm Michael Tallen, a contributing writer with the Herald…"

"We already get the paper," he interrupted.

"Uh, no, Sir, I'm not selling the paper. I'm here to see a woman named Ruth who called our office. She didn't give her last name; just said she wanted a writer to come to this address to take down her story as her dying wish."

"Dyin' wish? She ain't dyin'! That woman will outlive us all," he exclaimed, shaking his head and pushing the screen door open to let me inside.

I stepped into the entry and the little dog, a yorkie, uttered a soft growl while he sniffed my shoes.

"That's Bruiser. She don't bite. Of course, I can't say the same for Ruthie," he told me with a raised eyebrow and a serious expression. "Somebody get Ruthie and tell her she has a visitor!"

"Quit calling me that, and get outta my way," demanded an elderly woman, walking our way with the aid of a cane. She had grey hair cut short and styled a bit like Helen Mirren, and wore jeans with a white button-up shirt along with a strand of pearls and ruby red lipstick. Not at all what I expected, I braced myself for her examination of my appearance and blunt disapproval.

"You must be the writer from the Herald. Come on in," she invited.

I admit I was a bit shocked. Usually one look at my long, dark hair tied up in a "man-bun," my earrings and my tattoos; and people of a certain age would look at me with disgust and turn away. Not her. She didn't even flinch.

I followed her into a sitting room, and sat on an old, velvet couch that released a puff of dust and dog hair into the air.

"Can I offer you somethin' to drink?" she asked. She sat in a blue recliner across from me. Worn spots on the arm rests showed it had been used a lot.

"No, thank you. I was under the impression that having someone record your thoughts on your life was your dying wish, but the gentleman who answered the door indicated you're perfectly healthy."

"Well, I had to say something to get you here," she confessed. "I am eighty-nine years old, so I figure I'm closer to dying than most people. Call it 'creative truthing.'"

I chuckled and opened my notebook. I liked her spunk, and I figured anything she was so determined to say was worth recording.

"May I record this conversation?" I asked, pulling out my digital recorder.

"That's probably a good idea. We've got a lot of ground to cover. I can't expect you to memorize it all."

"A lot of ground, huh? Just what is it you're wanting me to write…your thoughts on life in general? A valuable lesson you've learned?"

"My story."

"Your story. As in your whole…life…story?"

"Yep. Well, the interesting parts anyway."

I cleared my throat. "Ma'am, first of all, I write short articles for the Herald about the arts and community events. I'm not a biographer. Second of all, the newspaper isn't the proper medium for sharing one's life story. They won't even consider publishing it…"

"I know all that! I've followed your work for a long time."

"Yeah, exciting stuff, isn't it?"

"There's been times…regardless, I want YOU to write my story." She seemed adamant. I had no idea why. I shifted in my seat and attempted to gather my thoughts. How could I convince her this was a horribly bad idea?

"Ma'am,"

"First of all, drop the Ma'am. Call me Ruth."

"Yes, m…Ruth. Uh…let's say I agree to write your story. Why is it so important to you to have it written? I mean, if you're wanting to pass down stories to your grandchildren, you could just have a family member write for you."

She stared at me with a slight grin, and we sat in awkward silence for a moment. I glanced around the room and noticed several framed black and white portraits in dusty, dark wooden frames. There were also what appeared to be framed newspaper clippings and photos of large animals, like elephants, hanging on the far wall. But, having forgotten to put in my contacts that morning, I couldn't make out any details.

"This isn't my house," she stated abruptly.

"It's not?"

"No. For the last fifteen years or so, this house was home to my dearest friend and cousin, Lizzie. We lived together as young girls on a farm in Ft.

Lauderdale, not too far from here." She looked away, seemingly lost in thought. "She passed away this week. I came here for her funeral."

"I sorry. My condolences."

"It was her time. She went peacefully. I guess that's the best any of us can hope for. Anyway, Lizzie had kept boxes upon boxes of letters, pictures, and other odds and ends from our time together. I've been sifting through those precious memories, and well…I think there's a story to tell in it all."

She had me hook, line and sinker. I sat there not knowing anything about this woman; not even if she was telling the truth, but completely convinced I should write for her. Her wrinkled hands rested folded in her lap, and her emerald green eyes nearly stared right through me; looking at me with anticipation.

"Alright then," I began, turning on the recorder, "where do we start?"

She clapped her hands together and smiled, "Wonderful. Let's begin! Oh, but not here. Let's go down the hall to Lizzie's room with all the boxes."

Grabbing her cane, she was up and walking, leading the way to the room full of memories. We stepped inside a small bedroom wallpapered in a pale yellow floral print reminiscent of a Chintz china pattern my grandmother once had. A white metal bed covered in an antique quilt sat against the middle of the back wall. A well-worn wingback chair sat near the window. A simple wooden dresser stood in a corner, and boxes of various sizes, including a few old, round hat boxes, were scattered throughout the room. A few boxes remained sealed, but most of them were open and their contents spilling out onto the bed or the floor.

"Pardon the mess. As I go through each box, my mind wanders to other times and far-away places, and I lose track of time...and any motivation to clean this stuff up."

"It's fine," I assured her, as I perched on the edge of the bed and picked-up a random photograph. It was a photo of a young girl, a teenager, with long hair tied with a ribbon, and holding a large feather in one hand. "This looks like it's from the late thirties, early forties, I'm guessing."

"Let me see." She took the photo from me and sat in the chair by the window. "Ah, yes. I was fourteen. So, that would be...um...nineteen and forty-one. Oh, yes, that's it...nineteen forty-one." She handed me back the picture.

"I can see it now...the cheekbones, the eyes."

"My heaven's...I'm a long way from that girl, now." She said as the corners of her mouth curled into a beautiful smile.

"Nah. She's still there. I see her."

She grinned, and I think she even blushed a little.

"Let's start here," I suggested. "Tell me about this picture, about you at fourteen, and about this feather."

Ruth leaned back in the chair and closed her eyes, and for a brief moment I thought she may had fallen asleep.

"Feathers have always been my favorite, and that one was a real prize. It was a tail feather from a hawk. Cyrus, one of the snake charmer boys, had found it and given it to me. I begged my mother to make me a sequined headband and attach the feather, but she refused. She didn't want me to look like the other girls around camp."

"Whoa, whoa, wait a minute. Snake charmer? Girls at camp?"

"Oh, I didn't tell you?"

"I don't think so. Tell me what?"

"Well, you see, Mr. Tallen…I was the lion tamer's daughter!"

***

After Ruth's exciting though somewhat bizarre revelation, she excused herself to "fetch a pot of tea" for the two of us. I slouched in my chair and surveyed the boxes of letters and pictures while questioning my sanity for remaining in the midst of such chaos.

This poor, delusional, old woman was intent on holding me hostage to listen to her ramblings about a fictional world. Or maybe not. Maybe she was telling the truth.

I grabbed the box closest to me, and reached inside; blindly grabbing whatever rested near the top. Submitting to my grasp were three photos and a folded letter. The first photo showed its age with muted tones and tattered edges; and pictured a teenage boy with a thin face and straight, dark hair.

He wore a long-sleeved shirt with ruffles down the front, tights and what appeared to be ballet shoes that rested on the back of an elephant. Quickly turning the photograph over, I read a penciled inscription on the back, "Albert and Pricha, 1941."

The other photos were of random people. They could have been friends or family, anyone really. And, I didn't dare read a personal letter without her consent. I stared at the picture of Albert, and realized Ruth might just be telling the truth…and it might be an amazing story that's worth hearing…and writing.

***

Ruth hobbled into the room shakily carrying a tray with a small tea pot and two cups with saucers. I swiftly rose to take the tray from her, and cleared a spot on the bed to set it down.

"I brought milk and sugar just like Maggie taught me when I was a girl."

"Who's Maggie?" I enquired as I discreetly pressed the record button on my digital recorder.

"She was one of the show girls, and she came all the way from London! She wasn't terribly talented, but she was beautiful, so Mr. Lewis found her a spot with the acrobats. She mostly stood and smiled and waved her arms about to direct the crowd's attention to what the acrobats were doing. Sweet girl though. She made good tea."

Ruth poured tea into our cups and allowed me to add sugar and milk to mine as I pleased.

"I think we're getting ahead of ourselves," I paused the recorder. "So far you've told me your father was the lion tamer, there was a girl from London in the show, and some man named Mr. Lewis was apparently in charge. This story is all over the place…mind starting from the beginning?"

"Not at all!" she replied as she leaned back in her chair, holding her cup and saucer in her trembling hands.

"Oh, and I definitely want to know who this is," I told her, handing her the photograph of Albert.

"Albert!" she exclaimed with a smile as she looked upon the photo. "You will most definitely hear about him!"

"Good. Alright then. Where are we starting? Year? Location?" I took the recorder off pause.

"Hmmm. Well, this may be the best place to start right here; where this picture of Albert was taken. It was 1941 in Bradentown, on our way to Sarasota."

"I believe you mean Bradenton," I corrected.

"No, I don't. I mean Bradentown, as it was called since 1903. It wasn't until 1943 that the state of Florida merged it with another town, and called it Bradenton."

Sharp as a freakin' tac. She got me. I cleared my throat.

"I stand corrected," I apologized. "Please continue."

She took a long sip of her tea. "As I was saying," she said, giving me a certain look. "We were camped in Bradentown. It was summer, and oh so hot..."

CHAPTER ONE

The temperature was in the nineties, and the humidity was near one hundred percent. Being circus folk who traveled primarily around the southern parts of the country, we were used to it; so no one complained really. It was part of the job. But, that being said, we had to be extra cautious to ensure everyone, animals included, drank enough water and had shade from the scorching sun.

So, my father being the gaffer, a manager of sorts, was running himself ragged around the camp. It was his duty to oversee the different acts and follow-up on their supplies, safety protocols and the like.

He had stopped by the wagon where the Martinelli family resided. The 'Marvelous Martinelli Acrobatic Family' were relatively new to our show. They were extremely talented, and just as extremely dysfunctional.

Mr. and Mrs. Martinelli were of Italian descent. They had four sons and three daughters ranging in ages from thirteen to twenty-four, and they all were involved in the act. Their second youngest, Albert, was fifteen. I was fourteen, and found myself quite smitten with him.

While the rest of his family tumbled and twirled on the ground, Albert chose to flip across the back of a juvenile elephant he had befriended, named Pricha. That's Thai for 'clever.' Pricha was indeed clever, as was Albert. His tricks on elephant-back were a crowd pleaser, and it made his father insanely jealous.

"Martinelli," my father called out. "Does Pricha have adequate shade and water?"

"Don't know and don't care. That stupid beast isn't my responsibility!"

"Fine. Then where's Albert? I'll take it up with him."

"He's probably out in a field somewhere practicing his act. I told him he couldn't practice with us anymore 'cause we need all our allotted time for our family act; not his showing off."

My father shook his head in disgust, but walked away silently. I observed him from the cook shack across the way where I was washing dishes; and I had so longed for him to throw a punch, or at least yell at the rotten man. But, my father chose the high road, as he called it, and set out to find Albert.

I managed to scrub the last pot from breakfast just in time to chase after my father. We cut through the big top, the largest tent for the big show and I cursed stepping in a pile of horse manure while trying to keep pace. Father walked quickly, casting dirt and manure every which way and never losing step. My eyes had not adjusted from leaving the bright Florida sun to the dark shade of the tent with small beams of sunlight piercing through holes and seams. I nearly ran into a rope supporting the trapeze, and got yelled at by one of the Baldocchi's, the trapeze family. Father caught sight of me, and gave me an annoyed look. I knew that look well.

"Ruthie! Hurry it up!" he hollered, as he waved me towards him.

I muttered a quick apology to the Baldocchi boy before running off. We stepped outside the tent and said hello to a group of showgirls sunbathing in the grass. I was so envious of their coiffed hair, their feminine bodies in off-the-shoulder tops and shorts, and their seemingly glamorous behavior of smoking cigarettes and sipping on soda in glass bottles through paper straws.

As for myself, I was a stick figure of a girl with my hair in a ponytail, wearing feed sack dresses and drinking from a tin cup from the mess tent.

Father interrupted my thoughts of self-pity. "Ruthie! Don't doddle!"

"Yes, Sir! If you're looking for Albert, you should try the field by the train tracks. There's a lot of room there for him to rehearse with Pricha."

"Well, good grief, Ruthie, why didn't you say so in the first place?"

"Because I was too out of breath from trying to keep up with you!"

Father chuckled and patted my head, but he didn't slow his pace any. We finally reached the train tracks and sure enough, there was Albert turning somersaults atop Pricha's back.

Albert had a lean, muscular build; and straight, dark hair that was too long in the front and fell across his forehead. While some performers hold their jaw tight and fix their gaze with concentration; Albert was relaxed, as if flipping backwards upon a giant beast while it walked around was as much a natural part of life as breathing. He and Pricha moved together effortlessly, more as lifelong friends than master and animal.

"Let's not disturb them," father spoke quietly. "But, didn't you want to check on Pricha's water?" I asked.

"That boy and his elephant are so bonded, there's no way he'd let Pricha go thirsty. I'm sure they're fine."

My father turned and walked away, but I lingered; observing Albert patting Pricha on the head and lying back to rest as if he were nestled in a hammock. Father was right. Those two had an amazing bond...and it made me a little jealous.

"I've got to see Mr. Lewis, and you know he doesn't like you hangin' 'round, not doin' anything."

I strongly protested. "But, I do plenty! I serve food and wash dishes every meal, and all my chores are done from breakfast. I still have time before I have to help with lunch…"

"Ruthie," he stopped, turned, and bent over to look me dead in the eye. "Not that your work isn't helpful, but Mr. Lewis has a bias against you because we don't force you to perform in an act or learn sewing to assist your mother, or follow in her footsteps."

"Why can't I follow in your footsteps?" Father laughed heartily. "A girl managing the circus? Directing the acts, taking control of tough situations, resolving conflicts, ensuring safety…"

"I'd be perfectly capable. I've watched you practically all my life. I know exactly what to do and how to handle people."

He straightened and his laughter and wide smile were replaced by silence and a slight smirk.

"We'll talk about this later. Go see if you can help your mother with anything," he instructed, and I obeyed.

He walked left towards Mr. Lewis' office, so to speak. I went right to walk through the backyard; that's what we called the area behind the big top where railroad cars were parked and smaller tents pitched for lodging performers and crew.

First, I passed by Arman and Cyrus, Arab brothers who perform in the side shows charming snakes, swallowing swords and breathing fire. Well, they don't really breathe fire. It's a trick. But, impressive nonetheless. They were lying back on blankets as if they were sunbathing, but their olive skin needed no help from the sun.

"Don't you have snakes to wrangle or somethin'?" I teased as I stepped between them.

"Do you not have dishes to wash...Ruthie?" Cyrus said, chuckling.

"Ugh! Don't call me that! My name is Ruth! You know I hate that!"

"Your father calls you Ruthie all the time..." added Arman, defending his brother.

"He's my father. He's allowed!"

"Are we not like your brothers?" asked Cyrus, sitting up and shielding his eyes from the sun with one hand.

"Yes, you are. Like big, annoying brothers!"

They both laughed and I kept walking through the yard.

Donald and Hank, our boss elephant men, were leading a small group of bull handlers to the train cars that housed the large animals. William, a new hired hand, was busily asking them questions, trying to retain as much information about his duties and expectations as he could.

A breeze blew through, providing respite from the heat. Unfortunately, it also blew up dirt and dust into my eyes. I stood still, wiping my eyes and blinking and even having a good sneeze, when I heard my name yelled from across the way.

"Ruth!" It was Norman, our ringmaster. Better known as "Normando the Great," he was ever the showman; eccentric and flamboyant, as a proper ringmaster should be. He had once worked for the revered Ringling Brothers, but settled for our smaller show because he was given more freedom to perform. At least, that's what he told everyone.

"Ruth, come over here!" he called to me from the steps of his living quarters, an antique circus wagon he insisted on having hauled around; as it had been in his family for generations. Well, that's what he told everyone.

"Come inside," he invited, and I followed after him.

It was the most ornately decorated tiny space I had ever seen. Nothing more than a bunk on one end and a small table with two chairs in the middle. But the whole thing was adorned with red velvet, gold filigree, and brass fixtures. I sat down at the dark wooden table across from Norman who had already set out two cups for tea.

"Maggie keeps telling me I should serve cream, but I think sugar is all one needs," he remarked.

"That's fine by me," I said, before taking a careful sip of the steaming hot liquid.

"I know it's hot out, but there's just something about a cup of hot tea that perks you up."

Norman waved his hands around as he spoke. My father joked privately that if he tied Norman's hands together, the man wouldn't be able to talk. Norman had no family that we knew of, so we went out of our way to be friendly; which meant I wouldn't be telling Norman about father's joke.

He was a tall man, about six foot two, and a little on the heavy side. He wore his silver hair in a pompadour style with a fancy moustache and beard; and wore excessive amounts of heavy gold jewelry— chains, rings, and bangles. He nearly always wore eyeliner and pink rouge on his cheeks. And, when not clothed in his ringmaster costume, he wore Oriental silk robes with matching slippers. This particular day, his robe was shades of green, which was my favorite color.

"I see you're admiring my robe," he said, having caught me staring and lost in thought.

"Yes, I do like it very much. Green is my favorite color."

"Green is a lovely color, and it is rare to find Oriental prints with so much of it. They tend to prefer reds and blues."

"The tea is delicious. Thank you," I said, trying to remember my manners.

"Glad you like it. Say, I just thought of something. You said you like green…sit right there." He got up, went to a shelf on the wall behind his bed, and pulled down a carved wooden box. Setting the box on the table, he winked at me, and opened the box.

"I've got a little present for you." Norman pulled out a small jade bracelet—a simple bangle of smooth jade and the prettiest shade of green I had ever seen. He slipped it onto over my hand, onto my wrist. "There! It looks beautiful on you. My hands are too fat for it," he said with a grin.

"It's lovely! Thank you so much." The clock struck ten, and I knew I had to get to mother before I had to go help with lunch. "I'd better go, but thank you...for everything."

Norman gave me a nod, and I scurried off to mother, glancing down every few seconds to admire my new piece of jewelry.

***

When I got to our quarters, mother was stitching a hole at the shoulder seam of a costume for one of the Baldocchi girls.

"I've got two more quick fixes that have to get done, and I'm behind on the new shawls and capes. Think you can handle a few easy stitches?" She asked.

Mother wasted no time in putting me to work. Sewing wasn't a talent I possessed nor a passion I pursued, but I did have minimal skill to help mother out when it was necessary.

"Yes, ma'am. I'll get to it."

The circus folk had two names for my mother, Mrs. Clarke and "creative genius." If I had a nickel for every time someone gazed upon one of my mother's designs with awe and declared her a "creative genius," I'd be rich beyond my wildest dreams. She could take a simple leotard; and with silk, embroidery, sequins and feathers, she'd turn it into a work of art.

Oh, but it didn't end there. She created headpieces, capes, and dressings for the animals that rivaled anything any other show had to offer.

Though my mother seemed to enjoy her craft, I always had the feeling that she had longed for bigger and better in her life; maybe to work in fashion in Paris or some such thing. But, first and foremost she adored my father and he was a circus man. So, she was a circus seamstress.

I watched her hands as she pulled thread and tied knots, and noticed how they'd aged. The thought came to me that I should learn from her in the event she could no longer sew as she did now; but I quickly dismissed the idea. That was not for me. My desire was to be like my father—be the boss, set the schedule, layout the camp, ensure everyone's safety, manage and supervise. That was the job for me! No more stirring pots of oatmeal or scrubbing pans. I'd put on my dress shirt and tie, pants and work boots; and dare anyone to say anything about my choice of attire. If we could have men with tattoos and strange piercings performing in our acts, we could have a woman in suit and tie managing the show!

"Ruthie," my father interrupted my train of thought. "When you're done with that, get to the cook shack in time to prepare lunch. I don't want meals running late."

"Yes, sir."

One day, I encouraged myself....one day.

***

Later that evening, as everyone was doing their final preparations for the show, I meandered through camp towards the Martinelli's living quarters. I had hoped to see Albert, and strike up a conversation; but as I drew near, I heard yelling.

"You gonna stop me, boy? I'm the man of this family, and I can drink all I want, I can do whatever I want, and still perform better than you and your stupid animal!"

"I'm sure you can, but for the sake of everyone's safety..."

Slap!

I gasped and I stood just a few feet from the entrance. Mr. Martinelli had been accused of becoming violent before, but no one had personally witnessed it other than his wife and one daughter who refused to speak against him.

"Get out and don't come back!"

Albert ran past me without a word, and I quickly walked toward home.

"Ruthie, walk with me," my father commanded, having spotted me hurrying by.

"Yes, sir?"

"I wanted to talk to you about what you said earlier—about wanting to follow in my footsteps."

"I know you don't approve."

"I never said that. Or, at least, I didn't intend to. But, there's more to my job than you realize. There's more to my footsteps, so to speak. I think it's time you heard the whole story; and maybe, when you hear it, you won't want to follow the path of my journey after all."

"Norman told me once that he's following in the footsteps of his father, grandfather and great-grandfather. They were all great and famous performers."

My father chortled. "Well…that's what he says."

He guided me through the backyard, and to a row of cages that held our lions, three males named Dillon, Kosey and Shir. Kristoff, the lion tamer, stood near the cages in full uniform with whip in hand.

"Everything checked?" my father asked Kristoff.

"Double-checked, and checked a third time myself…just like you taught me."

"Well done. Everyone looks calm; no pacing or signs of agitation."

"The boys have been well fed, and had plenty of nap time. We should have a great show."

Father nodded his approval, and stepped closer to one of the cages; appearing deep in thought and somewhat melancholy.

"Father? Are you alright?" I asked, concerned.

"Yes, Ruthie," he whispered. "Come here."

I stepped sheepishly towards him, and stood as close to his side as I could get.

"I haven't always been the gaffer. I started out assisting my father who was a boss elephant man."

"I've heard about him. He was great with the elephants."

"Yes, he was. He had a bond with them much like Albert has with Pricha. But, I had no such bond, and as I grew older, I didn't want to work with the elephants."

"What did you want to do?" I inquired.

"I was drawn to the lions. So, I was given my father's blessing to apprentice and become a lion tamer."

"You were a lion tamer?" I asked with intrigue. "I never knew that!"

"I know. That's because my time as a lion tamer did not end well."

"What do you mean?"

Father exhaled slowly and closed his eyes before he spoke again. "When you were an infant, we were putting on a show in a big city. The crowds were tough—not easily impressed by our small show.

So, to help sell tickets, I worked on a special trick with one of my lions, Othniel."

"Othniel? What kind of name is that?"

"It's a beautiful name...Hebrew for 'God's strength.' Anyway, Othniel and I were alone in the center ring. The other lions were removed so I wouldn't have to worry about a surprise attack while performing with Othniel. I opened his mouth and placed my head inside, resting my head on his tongue. Then, I removed my head from his jaws, he closed his mouth, and placed his front paws on my shoulders as if he was giving me a hug."

"That's amazing...except for the lion slobber."

"It was a crowd pleaser. But, while the audience was applauding and Othniel and I were taking our bows, a fire broke out in the grandstands. The tent ropes caught fire quickly, and it spread faster than anything I've ever seen. Before we knew it, the whole tent was in flames. Smoke filled the air, and people ran every which way trying to escape.

My assistant, Jim, came running to the cage to let me out, but I was trying to get Othniel back down the ramp and out of the tent, but it was still closed and locked."

"So, what did you do?" I questioned, eager to hear what happened next.

"I kept trying to force it open so Othniel could get to safety. But, the smoke was getting thick, and debris was falling upon us. My eyes burned and watered, and I became so hoarse from coughing that it was all I could do to speak. I told Jim we would have to open the door for me and Othniel—let him run where he could. Of course, he refused; knowing a lion on the loose would have only made the disaster even worse.

I stood still, trying to think of another option, but Jim and a couple of other men—I don't even remember who—opened the door, grabbed me and pulled me out...closing the door behind."

Father paused and removed his handkerchief from his pants pocket. He wiped his eyes and took a deep breath.

"They had to drag me out of that fire, kicking and screaming. We lost three good men in that fire along with Othniel. Men that worked to protect us, our animals, our livelihood."

"Oh, Father...I'm so sorry," I whispered, putting my arm around his waist and leaning against his arm.

"I mourned for weeks. I tried to go back into the ring with the remaining lions, but I never made it past the door. After several failed attempts, Mr. Lewis called me into his office. Mr. Dalton, our gaffer at the time, had been severely injured in the fire and was retiring; leaving to join his family in Georgia. So, I was offered the position as gaffer, managing the acts and setting-up safety protocols.

At first, even this was a difficult task. Everything reminded me of the night of the fire with all its trauma. But, over time, this job has been a way for me to heal. I get to look after the people and animals I care about, and ensure that no one is endangered like that again. Not a person…not a lion…or any other of God's creations."

"I understand."

"Do you, Ruthie? It's not just ordering people about and being a boss. It's not even about keeping a schedule or doing things a particular way. It's about looking after those you care about, and making sure everything works as it should for their sake."

I nodded and gave him a hug—as tight a squeeze as I could muster. Before either of us could say another word, Normando the Great began his introduction, and the Lewis Brothers Big Top Circus was underway.

CHAPTER TWO

"**That's a spectacular** beginning for a story," I told Ruth. "I've got great stuff to work with here, but I'm not sure all of what you're telling me is accurate."

"What makes you say that?"

"Well, you're giving me a lot of detail, and…no offense, but you are in your late eighties, and I'm not sure anyone could remember their past so…vividly."

Ruth gave me the nastiest look, as if I had just accused her of a heinous crime.

"Young man, I'll have you know," she spoke with fervor, "that I have a photographic memory. No, more than that. I can still remember the smells—the mix of sweet candy apples, fresh popped popcorn and unfortunately even the elephant manure. I remember the feel of the sudsy pots and pans in my hands. I remember the softness of his lips…"

"Lips? Now this story is getting' juicy."

Ruth glared at me. "That part of the story comes later, but only if you mind your manners."

"Yes, ma'am. You know, I can't stay here all day, as much as I'd like to. Maybe this would be a good stopping point. Let me listen to the tapes, take some notes, and come back to hear more."

"I think that's a fine idea," she said, softening her tone and giving me a grin.

"Alright, then. How about Wednesday? I think I have that morning available."

"I'll be here. I'm not going home for a couple of weeks. Too much to do 'round here."

We said good-bye, and I left for home; still reeling about the events of the day. Just how did I get picked to meet up with this extraordinary, old woman and hear her astonishing tale. She did say she had read my work, but really—what about local arts and society could she possibly have found interesting enough to want me to write about her life?

***

I walked down the sidewalk at a quick pace as I had suddenly remembered that I hadn't put nearly enough money in the meter for the amount of time I had ended up staying, listening to Ruth. Thankfully, my precious bike, a 1965 Triumph Bonneville, was still parked without so much as a chalk mark on the tire. Some good Samaritan had filled the meter, and I was thanking my lucky stars they did. When I first found Bonnie (yes, I named my motorcycle…get over it), she had been kept in a dilapidated shed, barely shielded from the Florida sun and salt air for over fifteen years. It took me an entire year and a sizable chunk of each paycheck to bring her back to life. Now, ol' Bonnie boasted a new leather seat; the trademark big, round gauges; British flags on the back shock absorbers; and a shiny chrome Triumph logo. She got me everywhere I needed to be. In return I kept her clean and purring like a kitten.

I drove to the Herald, housed in a pale yellow stucco box with white trim in desperate need of a paint job. It's a small outfit with just a few employees, but I preferred it to the big paper I worked for when I first started out—over a decade ago.

Normally, I'd enter quietly and work at my desk without as much as a hello from anyone else. Not that any of us are unfriendly; it's just that we all have jobs to do, and we prefer to stay focused on our individual tasks. But, today, I had a mission that required actual human interaction...as if I hadn't had more than my fair share today with Ruth. I headed straight to my editor's office and knocked hard on the door.

"Katz, you in there? I need to ask you..."

The door jerked open, and Katz waved me in as he spoke into his cell phone.

"Yeah, yeah, I hear ya. You want a fluff piece to make your guy look good. I tell ya what, double what you normally spend advertising with us and I'll have my writer make him sound like Micelangelo...
...(pause)...You've got 'til tomorrow morning. Get back to me." Katz hung up and fell into his chair. He rolled his eyes and tossed his phone on his desk.

Brian Katz was a fit fifty-year-old, tan and still blonde with a hint of grey. At first glance, one would think him an ol' surfer dude, but the man had degrees in journalism and marketing, a sophisticated wine pallet, and never surfed—just kayaked.

"These gallery owners are somethin' else," he complained. "They beg me to give their newest artist rave reviews, and try guilting me with all that 'support local business' talk. We're a local newspaper; we're a business; which means we're one of them! I bend over backwards to help these guys out, but we're a newspaper not the chamber of commerce." Katz picked up a pencil and started tapping it on his desk. "What's up, Mike?"

"Well, speaking of us being a newspaper," I attempted to segway, "why on earth did you send me to this old lady who wants her life story written?"

Katz practically howled. "She sounded so wacky over the phone, I just had to do it! What I'd give to see the look on your face when she started talking!"

"Ha. Ha. Very funny," I replied dryly, taking a seat across from his desk.

"Seriously, though. She asked for you specifically and wouldn't give a reason other than you 'were the one.' Like Neo in the Matrix or something."

I leaned back in my chair and crossed my legs and arms. "Well, smart guy, as it turns out, she is truly fascinating and has quite a story to tell. I'm going back Wednesday to hear more. It's just that there's no way we can print this in the paper. Of course, I'm pretty sure her intention all along was to get me to write it as a book or something."

"You ought to! I mean, if she's as interesting as you're implying…could be a great opportunity. How many journalists become bestselling novelists?"

Now I laughed. "Right. I think you're getting ahead of yourself. I have to actually write this, and then see if anyone besides Ruth and her family even want to read it! Anyway, you say she asked for me specifically? That's just weird. She did say she'd read my work…"

"She sounds like an odd old bird. Who knows? Now, get outta of my office. I've got work to do."

"Like extorting art galleries for favorable reviews?"

"Out! Go write something!" Katz said tossing his pencil towards me. It whizzed by my head.

As I was leaving his office, I turned to close the door behind me and a thought occurred to me.

"Wednesday night, after my next meeting with Ruth. You should come over to listen to the tapes. I'll serve wine."

"You drink that cheap stuff. I'll bring the wine. Now, get!" He ordered, looking for another projectile to lob my way.

***

After an hour or so of sorting my notes from the day's adventure with Ruth, I headed home to my own stucco box—an off-white version, built in 1955. Not a fancy house, but just fine for yours truly. Two bedrooms, one bathroom, a little kitchen, and two large oak trees in the back yard that shaded the six by nine concrete slab I called my patio. The only real amenity was that I resided within walking distance of a bike trail that I journeyed regularly on board my vintage Schwinn.

Unable to shake loose from thoughts of Ruth's story, I hit play on the recording our conversation, and settled back in my thrift store pleather recliner with a bottle of hard lemonade. As much as I hated to admit it, this assignment, as it were, had intrigued me.

After listening for a while, I got up and rummaged in the fridge for the leftover Chinese food from few nights before. I gave it the sniff test. Seemed fine. I nuked it in the microwave. Then I sat back down with my chow mein and listened more intently.

Ruth was recalling her tea time visit with Normando, the ringmaster. I begrudgingly pulled out my laptop and started typing. Suddenly Wednesday couldn't get here fast enough.

***

Wednesday actually arrived quicker than I had anticipated. Up at seven, I pulled my hair up on top of my head and oiled my beard--feeling more like a well-coiffed Viking than a journalist—and threw my recorder and notepad in my backpack.

Bonnie started right up and, as was typical of my adored ride, she led me to the closest coffee shop. Ninth Bar Coffee makes my favorite morning beverage; liquid energy called the Double Dog Espresso. I figured if I was going to sit in an old, dusty house surrounded by antiques, and listening to an ol' woman tell me about her childhood, I should have plenty of caffeine to get me through it. Who was I kidding? That was just the lame excuse I gave myself for giving in to my biggest vice (besides the occasional tattoo). I was stoked to hear more about the circus family and Ruth's childhood love interest. But, still…coffee is a must.

Omar waved hello to me as I walked in, and I gave a courteous nod to the giant pink octopus that adorns the wall behind the bar. Personally, I think her name should be Octavia, but I would never suggest naming a mural; they might think I'm nuts. I don't know what it is, but ever since I was a kid, I've assigned names to things—especially things I like. I jokingly told the barista that I double-dog dared her to give me a double dog espresso, and she giggled. She was cute, but young. Probably early twenties. Once I passed thirty, I gave up pursuing girls like her. Lately, I hadn't pursued anyone…except now I was in pursuit of a ninety-year old woman with a crazy past.

Downing my last sip of that glorious concoction, and wishing I could take another cup with me, I headed out to meet Ruth. Once there, Bruiser yipped and growled at me with the upmost disdain before finally letting me step inside the door. Ruth led me to the same room where had met before, and I noticed the boxes were more carefully stacked and seemingly organized.

"I found a few pictures that might help you visualize my story," Ruth said as she motioned towards a small box on the bed.

"Your story-telling is so rich and detailed; I haven't really had much trouble envisioning the places or the people."

"Thank you. I tried to convey all the details as best I could."

She handed me a cup of hot tea that didn't really appeal to me, but I took it anyway. I set the recorder on the bed, and picked up the top picture from the stack inside the little box. The black-and-white image was of a middle-aged man with deep wrinkles, a salt-and-pepper moustache, and dark circles under. his eyes. He wore a well-tailored suit and a scowl, as if he wasn't happy his picture was being taken.

"Who's this?" I asked as I handed Ruth the picture.

"Oh, that's Mr. Lewis. He and his brother owned the circus. They were partners until George passed away suddenly from an apparent heart attack. After that, Frank kept to himself as much as possible and mostly let father run the show. Come to think of it, this would be a good place to get back to our story…"

CHAPTER THREE

Our little circus traveled around the southeast while the weather was good, but even the south can get nasty winter storms. So, every winter we packed up after our final show of the season and headed to the Volusia County fairgrounds in Florida. Mr. Lewis had an arrangement that allowed us to use the fairgrounds and its buildings and barns for housing our equipment, animals, and even some of our crew.

Some of the families, the performers, went other places to stay with relatives. We always went with the circus, and my father would work on a local farm, along with other migrant workers, for the season. Mother would make dresses and do embroidery work for some of the more well-off ladies in town. I would help at the childcare facility that watched over children of the farm hands while their parents worked.

In 1941, we had a long trek to get to Volusia for the winter. Our final show had been up near Louisville, Kentucky. We had over eight-hundred miles to cover in our train cars and trucks—with children and animals that needed frequent stops. Normally our vehicles would ride the train, secured to flatbed cars. But, for this trip, we split into two groups. My family rode along in a caravan of trucks and travel trailers with other circus families while the animals and a lot of our equipment were hauled by the train, along with the crew.

We were only a few hundred miles into our journey when stopped at a little store for some snacks and drinks. Mr. Martinelli, Albert's father, was already somewhat intoxicated. He purchased some beer and staggered as he carried it back to his truck. His wife rushed to help him, and Albert said something he shouldn't have; I don't know what exactly. Mr. Martinelli turned towards Albert and whipped off his belt faster than anything I'd ever seen. He ran towards Albert swinging that belt, and Albert took off towards a group of trees next to the store. Fortunately, Mr. Martinelli was so drunk, he stumbled and fell which allowed Albert to get away. That man lied there cussing and fussing; then he struggled to get his feet while he screamed at his wife and yelled out to Albert.

"Get back here! I'm gonna whip your…"
Bam!
Everyone's heads turned toward the sound. Mr. Lewis stood there by the Martinelli's truck with a baseball bat in his hand, and a sizable dent above the back wheel.

"What'd ya do that for? You gonna ruin my truck!" Mr. Martinelli complained.

"I'm gonna ruin your kneecaps if you don't leave that boy alone. Kinda hard bein' a gimp acrobat. Now, get in the back of the truck and sober up while your wife drives." There was a moment of silence. "I ain't askin'." Mr. Lewis clarified.

Mr. Martinelli quietly shuffled to the truck and hopped into the bed along with their belongings. His wife got in the driver seat with Albert's brother holding one sister on his lap and another sister beside him.

"You, come with me," Mr. Lewis instructed Albert. "You shouldn't be riding in the bed of a truck."

"You got me riding in the bed of a truck!" yelled Mr. Martinelli.

"And that's better than you deserve!"

Mr. Lewis gave the truck another smack with the bat, and Mr. Martinelli shut right up. That was the last time I ever saw Mr. Lewis act as the boss. Anytime a boss was required, he had my father handle it.

***

When we arrived at the fairgrounds, the first thing to do was to find our assigned quarters and move in our belongings. Once the train arrived, we would have to help with the animals and equipment.

We had a small groundskeeper house near the back of the grounds that was unfortunately in close proximity to the barn where the elephants would be housed. That meant that a breeze in our direction would carry a stench along with it. I wasn't too bothered, though, because I had big plans that would keep out of that tiny house for most of the winter break. I had money to earn, fields to explore and a boy to rescue.

I determined in my mind that I could convince my father to make arrangements for Albert; maybe he could stay with us or with another family. He just needed away from his no-good father. Of course, the fact that I was enthralled with Albert would have made it awkward should he have stayed with us, but I wasn't thinking about that. I wanted to rescue the boy I adored.

I helped mother put sheets on the beds and set-up her sewing machine. Then I skipped down the dirt service roads all the way to the train tracks to watch for the train. Albert was already there, anxiously awaiting the arrival of his beloved Pricha. He was oblivious to my presence as he walked along the tracks, watching his own feet move across the grass. Suddenly a whistle bellowed and we both looked for the train. It was still a-ways off, coming around the bend; but the chug of its engine shook the ground. I walked towards Albert in hopes of speaking to him concerning my plan, but he bent over to pick something up and came towards me with an outstretched hand.

"For you," he said as he handed me a beautiful red feather. "From a cardinal...a male. Only the males have red like that."

I held the feather close to observe its beauty, and was too enamored with the gift to even thank him. Albert ran past me, following the train to where it would stop to unload the rest of our circus family. I just stood there holding my feather with a racing pulse and sweaty palms. Maybe this meant he liked me.

***

First off the train were the crew, followed by the horses and dogs. When it was time to unload the elephants, a large reinforced ramp was by the train car doors. It took six men to carry the ramp, and two men to slide open the heavy metal doors. As the door slid open, metal scraping against metal and chains banging against the car wall; Pricha stuck her trunk out as if gasping for air. She nearly fell down the ramp, and every man standing by ran to her side. They carefully guided her down the ramp while Albert demanded to know what was wrong with her and placed his hand behind her ear.

"She's trembling! What did this stupid train do to her? Did any of you look after her?" Albert's voice cracked as he yelled at everyone around him. In that moment, he reminded me of his father the way he screamed; only Albert was acting out of concern and not malice.

Donald and Hank helped Albert lead Pricha down the ramp and under a group of palm trees providing a little shade. William, the newest member of the crew, was sent to fetch water in case the poor beast had somehow become dehydrated. No one seemed to know anything for sure; only guesses based on years of experiences with animals. Father showed up within minutes, having been retrieved by Albert's sister Maria.

"Any idea what's going on?" Father asked.

"We thought maybe dehydration, but she isn't drinking…at least not much," replied Hank.

"What about it, Albert? You know this elephant better than anyone."

I could the deep concern on Albert's face.

"I don't know. She's yawning a lot, and her belly keeps moving like she's breathing hard. I just…don't know," he declared hopelessly as he wiped away tears.

"Alright, then. I'll place a call to the doc."

Father always hesitated calling in a veterinarian. For one thing, they seldom knew anything about large, exotic animals—mostly working with cats and dogs. And, for another, they almost always implied we, the circus, were mistreating them. Nothing could be further from the truth. Yes, there were shows who mishandled the majestic creatures under their care; but we were not one of those. We loved our animals as family.

Lucky for us, there happened to be a brand new veterinarian in town who specialized in larger animals like horses and cattle. He would at least have a better working knowledge that could benefit our situation.

Doc Turner was tall and lean, almost skinny. He had salt and pepper hair that sat fluffily on top of his head, and a large moustache that curled on the ends. He was pleasant, and greeted my father kindly with a firm handshake. Father always said he could tell a good man by the firmness of his handshake.

Doc Turner looked Pricha over for just a few minutes. "She's got mucous dripping, and see how rapidly her breathing is?" he said, placing Albert's hand on her side.

"I noticed that," Albert said, nodding.

"Is she resisting movement?"

"Yes, Sir. She didn't want to walk over here. We practically had to force her. And she won't lie down. She drank a lot at first, but then wouldn't drink anymore."

The doctor placed his hand on his chin and continued observing the elephant, deep in thought. "I don't see any signs of parasites or rat bites. I think she may have pneumonia. Has she been overworked or under stress for a while?"

"She doesn't particularly like the train ride," admitted Donald. "We kept her separate from the other elephants to give her more space since this was a longer trip than normal."

"You came from up north—here to winter?" asked the doctor.

"Yes, Sir."

"Was she exposed to cold and wet conditions before you left?"

"Just a little, but we kept her under as many blankets as we could," said Albert.

"It's most likely pneumonia. There's not a lot we can do, medication wise, but I do have a treatment plan that seems to work. I treated two of Ringling's elephants for pneumonia this way and they both recovered."

"Tell us what to do, and we'll see to it right away," father assured him.

"Keep her separated from the others. Provide her shade and ample water. She'll start drinking again, and she'll be extra thirsty. Feed her ripe bananas, fresh grass, and if you can get it, sugarcane. She's gonna have to fight this off on her own, but we can support her as she does."

Father sent Hank and William to find bananas and sugarcane, and assigned Donald to stay with Albert and Pricha. Knowing that Doc Turner had been successful with other elephants gave all of us hope and confidence that our beloved pachyderm would be well again soon.

While most of our circus family that wintered together worked as farm hands, two of our brothers-by-bond found unique work. Arman and Cyrus, the resident snake charmers, were obviously skilled in the handling of snakes. All of Florida had its share of snakes, but this particular year and location seemed to have slithery creatures in abundance.

With coral snakes, diamondback and pygmy rattlers; the boys had plenty of work wrangling them from of bunk houses, outhouses and even amongst the crops if too many workers had suffered bites or close calls. Plus, there was a rattlesnake meat factory in Tampa, not too far away. Since they couldn't keep dead snakes cool enough to stay fresh, they kept most of their snakes alive in boxes until they reached the factory.

Riding around in a beat-up, black, '38 pickup truck on loan from the circus, the pair of brothers traveled farm to farm, ridding them of dangerous snakes and taking advantage of the surplus population of young, attractive women. With their olive complexion, dark hair and eyes and bright smiles; the handsome pair captured both the attention and affection of most females.

On one particular day, Arman and Cyrus spent two hours tracking down and catching a black racer.

It wasn't a poisonous snake, but it moved very quickly and startled the women and children.

Not wanting his workers to fear being in the fields, the farm owner hired the brothers to get rid of the animal. Having caught it, they placed it in a pillow case and tied the top closed. Proud of their success, they swaggered through the rows of housing; waving, smiling and holding up the wiggly pillow case for all to see. The girls were so impressed and very grateful—and they had never seen Arab men before, so they found the brothers very exotic and enticing. "You are now safe!" exclaimed Arman. "We caught the terrifying creature, and will take him far away from here."

"Why don't you just kill it?" asked a little snotty-nosed boy, about six years old.

"Because he eats rats! And if he didn't eat the rats, the rats would come in and make you all sick. Snakes are not all bad, my friend," explained Cyrus.

"I'd still kill it," said the boy as he walked back to his mother.

Feeling like they were losing the admiration of the residents, Arman decided to take action. He untied the pillow case, and reached in to grab the snake. Normally, he would grab just behind the head to avoid getting bit, but he wasn't careful enough and the snake bit him between his thumb and forefinger. Arman yelled, and in return, all the girls standing nearby yelled and ran away. He shook the snake off onto the ground, and the racer quickly made its escape under one of the bunk houses.

"What did you do that for?" Cyrus demanded.

"I was just going to show them the snake, but he bit me!"

"Why were you going to show them the snake? They didn't ask to see it!"

"Why aren't you concerned about my wellbeing? I've been bit!"

"By a black racer...it's harmless!"

"It doesn't feel so harmless!" Arman retorted.

"Now we've gotta crawl under there to find it," stated Cyrus, looking at the small space between porch floor and the ground. "You first."

Arman's eyes widened. "Me? Why me? I'm injured!"

"You're the one who let the snake go! And, you're hardly injured."

Arman started to argue his defense a little more, but realized it wouldn't do anything but take up valuable time and daylight. He conceded with a punch to Cyrus' arm, and crawled under the porch to retrieve the escaped reptile.

***

After all the excitement with Pricha and the veterinarian, and then Arman coming back with a

snake bite on his hand; I had almost forgotten my own event of the day—Albert gave me a feather!
I found Mother doing some embroidery for a fancy dress she was making one of the ladies in town.
It was a floral design; leaves of bright green with red flowers outlined in gold—all along the front of the waist of the navy fold-over collar dress.

"Momma, did you hear about Pricha?"

"Yes, Ruth. Your father told me she should be fine in a few days…thanks to the new doctor in town."

"Yes, ma'am. And did you hear about Arman and Cyrus and the black snake?"

"I did. I gave them some scraps of fabric to use as bandages, and for tying up pillow cases. I also warned Arman about trying to show off."

I laughed. "He does like attention."

Mother smirked. "He likes the attention of all those girls. What's that in your hand?" she asked, nodding towards the feather in my grasp.

"I was just about to tell you! It's a cardinal feather…or, well, I think it is. Albert said it was. He gave it to me!"

Mother stopped her needlework. "Let me see."
I stepped closer and held out the feather for her to examine.

"I believe he's right; though I'm no bird expert. It is a lovely color. Reminds me of my favorite poem…one your grandmother used to recite."

"Please tell me!" I begged.

"I don't recall the whole thing—just the first lines…something like 'Hope is that thing with feathers that perches upon the soul.'"

"What does it mean?"

"If I remember correctly, the poem describes hope as a songbird that cheers the soul and warms the heart. Maybe we can find the poem in a book at the schoolhouse, and we can read it and understand. It's been many years since I've read Emily Dickinson."

"Is that who wrote it?"

"It is."

"I wonder what she hoped for."

"I don't know that she ever says—not in her poem anyway. What do you hope for?"

I thought about my hope that Albert would fall in love with me, but I didn't dare confess that!

"Oh, just that Pricha gets better. That's all," I lied.

***

CHAPTER FOUR

"**I can't believe** you told a fib," I teased Ruth.

"It was just a little white lie. I really did want her to get better! Besides, lying is telling an untruth. I simply didn't reveal all the information."

"To quote Emily, 'Tell all the truth, but tell in slant.'"

Ruth grinned and clapped her hands together. "Bravo! You know Emily Dickinson's poetry!"

"Yes, ma'am. I'm a secret fan of hers," I admitted.

"Secret? Why secret?"

"Poetry isn't exactly…masculine."

"Michael Tallen, you're a hypocrite," she scolded me.

"What? Why?"

"You wear earrings."

I howled with laughter. "Touché!"

"William Shakespeare, Walt Whitman, Robert Frost…" she began rattling-off with the speed of an auctioneer.

"Yes, yes, I know. Men can write poetry."

"And recite it! It's actually quite charming," she said with a blush before taking her last sip of tea.

"It's just a hang-up of mine. I prefer to keep my poetry love private."

"But you shared it with me." She smiled, and dabbed a napkin at the corners of her mouth.

"Yes, well, you're sharing your whole life story. I owe you something in return."

"Do a good job writing my story—that's all I ask."

"No worries there. This story practically writes itself."

"Have you begun writing?"

"I have. And speaking of writing, I've got a newspaper assignment to work on; so I'd better be going." I began gathering my belongings together.

"I understand. Maybe you could come again this weekend? We haven't gotten very far. Perhaps I should skip ahead a little."

"Maybe...but you have to tell me if Pricha survives or not."

"I promise I will, but not today. Always keep them wanting more, as Normando used to say."

"So we end today with a cliff-hanger. I can live with that."

I stood and carried the tray of tea cups to the kitchen before making my way to the door.

"You have a lovely afternoon, Ruth."

"You, too, Michael dearest," she said with a wink.

***

I tossed my backpack across my back as I straddled Bonnie for the ride to the office. Like any woman, she has a mind of her own, and she drove me right back to 9th Bar for another round of coffee.

"Back again so soon?" Omar asked, feigning shock.

"It's Bonnie. She insists on coming here," I said nodding towards my bike parked just outside the door.

"She has good taste!"

After a perfect cup of espresso, I insisted Bonnie get me to work; which she did, in record time.

***

My newest assignment was a piece on the upcoming Jazz Holiday Music Festival that happened the second week of October. This four-day event was one of my favorites, and this year the Commodores were performing. In the past, I had been fortunate to hear Gladys Knight and the Count Basie Orchestra—some of my favorites. It wasn't that I was disinterested in the event; it was that I wasn't interested in writing about it. Nothing about it had the intrigue of Ruth's story. Nothing about it had the excitement of an investigative piece, like I used to write years ago. I was beginning to realize that the thing I ran away from was the thing I missed the most.

***

After plucking away at an article about the music festival, I gave up trying to build any enthusiasm and headed home. The evening air was starting to feel cool as if we actually experienced a real autumn in the sunshine state.

On the way home, I went through a drive-thru and grabbed a burger and fries; making a mental note to get back to eating healthy and working out, sometime in the near future.

I pulled up to my house to realize I had forgotten to leave a light on. Fumbling with my keys to unlock the door in the dark took what felt like forever. Finally, inside, I tossed my stuff onto the kitchen table, a vintage card table with metal legs I found at the flea market; and went to the fridge for ketchup and a can of soda.

I decided to listen through the day's recording with Ruth; so I took my food to the coffee table and sat in my comfy chair. It had been months since I left the city to this smaller, more intimate location. Yet, I hadn't made a single new friend nor had I kept in touch with old ones. Here I sat with fast food in my scarcely furnished house with no one else around, and only my recording of Ruth to keep me company. Pathetic.

Ruth spoke so fondly of the friends of her past, her circus family. Something about her story rekindled a desire within me to connect with humanity once again. Interviewing gallery owners and local artists was easy to do at arm's length. Bantering with a barista only required wit, not relationship. Getting to know someone and their history, like with Ruth, required an actual connection and real interaction. I thought I was done with people. I had been convinced I didn't even like people anymore. But, now...

"Ruth, what have you done to me?" I asked, speaking to an empty room.

***

Ruth and I had agreed to start our meeting at eight-thirty Saturday morning. Knowing I would be hard-pressed to function that early on a weekend, Bonnie drove me to 9th Bar for a double espresso before arriving at Ruth's house—well, actually, Ruth's late cousin's house.

This time Ruth had a tray of tea ready for us on the back porch. Thankfully, it was screened-in to protect us from the pterodactyl-sized mosquitos. The view was, unfortunately, of the back yard, filled with potted plants in varying stages of life and lifelessness. No rhyme or reason to the landscaping, miscellaneous lawn furniture strewn about, and a dilapidated wooden fence gave the area "podunk panache."

I sat in a folding lawn chair that almost folded-up when I sat down, and set the recorder on a glass-top metal table—actually more rust than metal—that sat between myself and Ruth who was comfortably nestled into a gliding chair with pillows.

"Oh dear! You can't sit in that!" she exclaimed once she noticed my sitting predicament.

"I can make it work," I lied.

"No, no, it won't do at all. Eddie! Fetch my guest a decent chair!"

Eddie, the same gentleman who greeted me the first time I came, carried out a wooden chair from the dining room, complete with red velvet upholstery.

"Better?" Ruth asked.

"Oh, yes…better. Thanks." Clearly, I was endangering my spot in heaven with all this lying. Maybe I'd bring my own folding chair next time.

Ruth scratched her forehead acting as if she was having trouble remembering something. "Now, if I recall—and I usually do—we agreed to skip ahead a bit." She certainly liked to rub it in.

"Yes, but you promised to tell me if Pricha survived." I said, acting as if I hadn't noticed her little jab.

"Well, I will just tell you that she did. She pulled through after six days of the doctor's treatment."

"I'm sure Albert was relieved!"

"He was overjoyed. But, his joy didn't last long. That no-good father of his stirred up trouble again; and this time, things did not end well."

CHAPTER FIVE

Everyone had settled into the routine of "normal" work and the change of life the winter season brings. Though each of us preferred the fast pace of the circus circuit—with the exception of mother, I think—we all accepted these few months for what they were; a time to be still and live as the rest of the world.

The Martinelli girls babysat, helped canned preserves, and did light sewing such as mending holes and attaching buttons. The older boys worked on nearby farm. Their mother worked in the fields, but their father had decided to look for more "respectable" work in town. Every evening he'd come home drunk after supposedly spending his day going door to door of local businesses.

One memorable night, Mrs. Martinelli had reached her limit with his foolishness. As her husband stumbled across the dirt road headed towards their tent behind one of the bunkhouses, she ran out to meet him with a bucket of cold water and doused him good.

"Woman!" he screamed. "What do you think you're doing?"

"I'm waking you from your intoxication! This is the last time you'll come home drunk or you'll find your home empty! No more goin' to every bar in town. You'll work here with me or you'll live without me!"

Albert heard the commotion from the elephant barn, and ran towards his parents. Just as he approached the road, he witnessed his father pull back his fist and swing at his mother's face; knocking her to the ground.

Albert lost all control, and ran full force to his father; jumped on his back and punched him over and over 'til Mr. Martinelli flipped him over his head and onto the ground. By now, several of us were standing at our doors; watching this drama unfold by the pale yellow light of a single streetlamp.

"You no good piece of…"

"Piece of what? Go ahead. Say it!" Albert challenged. He was lying in the mud glaring at his louse of a father.

Mr. Martinelli spit blood from his busted mouth onto the road where it mixed with dirt and sand. "You, boy," he pointed at Albert, "weren't wanted—wasn't supposed to be here. I hit your momma's stomach to stop you from comin', but you persisted. You showed up and 'bout near killed her. She wasn't conscious enough to name you so the nurse made me come up with somethin'. I took a pinch from my can of Prince Albert tobacco, and told her 'Albert Prince Martinelli!'"

He told this story with wild and loose gestures; waving his arms about and pausing only to light a cigarette and chuckle with his own delight in having humiliated Albert. "You ain't no prince; that's for sure. That ol' nurse asked if I was serious, and I told her it didn't matter what we named you 'cause we wouldn't be keepin' you if I could help it."

Albert sat on the ground now holding onto his mother, sobbing and clenching his fists; listening to his father spill his venom.

"You've been a thorn in my side since before you were born. Now you've got your momma tryin' to order me around and act like she's somethin' special. Forget her. Forget you." Mr. Martinelli looked around at all the circus folk standing there like sideshow spectators. "Forget all of you!"

With one last spat on the ground towards his own wife and son, Mr. Martinelli walked back down the road toward town, and faded into the darkness of night. We never saw him again.

***

Thanksgiving day, the meal tent was all set up fancy with nice china supplied by Normando. I loved the beautiful blue, flowery pattern on the plates, bowls and cups. Father and Mr. Lewis had went into town and came back with three large turkeys and more canned goods, bags of produce and soda bottles than I had ever seen in my entire life. Everyone pitched in and helped with cooking and setting the table, Normando happily pointing and barking out directions. He was always on. A natural ringleader.

One of the trapeze girls, named Camilla, made a sweet potato casserole that was to die for. I even tried some fried rattle snake meat at the behest of Armand. It wasn't too bad. As cliché as it sounds, it tasted like chicken. Judging from his expression I think he was impressed that I actually ate it. The sight of our circus family working and laughing together is one of my most cherished memories.

While we were sitting around eating our delicious dinner I noticed the Martinelli's at the far end of my table. Albert whispered to his mother. She nodded and Albert grabbed his plate and drink and walked down to where I was. He asked if he could sit next to me. My heart swooned but I played it cool and told it was okay with me if he wanted to.

"How are you?" Albert asked.

"Good. And you?"

"Good."

"That's good."

Our stimulating conversation went on like that throughout the rest of our meal. When we were done Albert asked if I'd like to go with him to give Pricha some of the food. She had quite the sweet tooth and we took her two whole pumpkin pies. She must've liked them because they were gone in about forty five seconds. We talked as we walked back to the tent and helped with the clean-up. With that done everyone said their goodnights and went home. That was a good day.

There was so much food we had leftovers for three days. That may not seem like a big deal but when you consider there were some thirty five mouths to feed…that is a lot of food.

After the holiday had passed, we all slipped back into our winter routine; working our jobs on farms and in town, gathering all together one evening a week for a meal. There was one noticeable absence. Normando had left the day after Thanksgiving to go and visit with some family he had that lived about an hour and a half away. We all missed his boisterous voice and endless supply of colorful stories. Sometimes they were so funny I'd spit my food out.

***

One day, the Martinelli family was rehearsing some new stunts without their father, and were discovering they were perfectly capable of wowing a crowd all on their own. Albert was even pulling some double duty helping out with putting their act together as well as practicing his own with Pricha.

One day I watched as they went through their routine. Their movements were so graceful and elegant I was in awe of their talent. When they finished I applauded and did my best to whistle.

Albert, the official showoff of the group, took a few extra bows. He then did about four front flips and landed right in front of me. I jumped back out of reflex and fell off of the bleacher seat. Albert was frozen.

"You okay, Ruth?!" He asked, almost afraid to move again.

"All except my pride," I answered.

Once he realize I wasn't hurt, Albert laughed until tears ran from his gorgeous eyes. He helped me up and dusted me off. If only he'd known that I had begun to fall for him way before that day.

***

A couple of weeks had passed since Thanksgiving and one day I was out with mother. I was helping her deliver completed dresses to ladies in town, when an unexpected visitor arrived. We were walking along the sidewalk down a residential street lined with little pastel houses and palm trees, when we suddenly heard a car honking its horn repeatedly.

Heading the opposite direction, towards town, was an old red truck pulling an ornately decorated circus wagon, driven by…Normando! As soon as I recognized him, I jumped up and down, waving my arms over my head.

"Normando! It's you! What are you doing here?" I ran across the street with mother following behind, and reached inside the truck window to hug Normando's neck.

"I decided I like my circus family more than my blood relatives," he said with a chuckle.

"I'm so glad you're here! Please say you're staying at the fairgrounds."

"I plan on it! I'm heading there now to set up my camp. You can come over later, and we'll have tea."

I looked at mom and gave her my best puppy dog eyes in an effort to get her permission.

"Fine by me!" she approved. "But you've got to help me get these dresses delivered quickly."

"Yes, ma'am!"

"Alright, you get moving and help your mother. I'll see you later," and with two beeps of the horn, he was trucking down the road.

***

Mother and I had delivered all but one of the dresses. I was so anxious to finish so I could go have tea with Normando that I about drove mother nuts with my constant chatter and lightning-quick steps.

"I know we're in a hurry, but you simply must calm down, Ruth. You're wearing me out!"

Our final stop was the home of Mr. and Mrs. Frost. Mr. Frost was a county judge and his wife, Geraldine, was a socialite known for her parties and fundraising for charities. She had commissioned mother to make an emerald green taffeta evening gown with a hand-pleated bodice and fitted waist that blossomed into a full, ankle-length skirt. It was gorgeous enough to be worn on a red carpet in Hollywood.

Mrs. Frost was an attractive woman who had won many beauty pageants in her youth. She had been sought after by multiple bachelors; but being as smart as she was pretty, chose the man with the best career potential—a young, up and coming lawyer and politician.

Mr. Frost wasn't the best looking, but he certainly became the best provider any woman could ask for. Their household boasted the latest amenities and luxuries, and their wardrobe was second to none. Mother felt honored to make dresses for Mrs. Frost, knowing her eye for beauty and quality and her desire to dress to impress.

The Frosts' maid saw us walking up while she swept the front porch.

"I'll fetch the lady of the house," she called out to us before running inside.

We stood on the porch of the white, Greek revival house with its black shutters and a second story balcony from the master bedroom. I could just imagine it all lit up at night—a bustle of activity with guests and music flowing as steadily as the wine.

"Helen, dear, come in!" Mrs. Frost invited, interrupting my imaginings of her social soirées.

We stepped just a few feet inside, then mother stopped and unwrapped the dress she had carefully folded and covered in butcher paper in order to keep it clean. The skirt unfurled from her arms and touched the floor in a cascade of shiny green.

"Oh, it's exquisite!" Mrs. Frost declared, placing her hands to her face.

"I'm glad you're pleased. It would be good for you to try it on and make sure the fit is right. That way I can make any needed alterations in time for your party."

"Come with me," Mrs. Frost motioned for mother to follow her. Mother, in turn, motioned for me to stay put.

I was admittedly a bit perturbed, as I had wanted to see the house—especially the bedroom with its four-post bed, luxurious linens and chandeliers. Instead, I glanced around me at the floral wallpaper, shiny wood floors and a fancy round marble-top table with the largest bouquet of flowers I had ever seen. Before I mustered up any courage to peek beyond the table, mother arrived with a smile on her face, and shooed me out the door.

"Where's the dress?" I asked.

"She's still wearing it. Fit her like a glove!"

"So, that's it? We're leaving?"

"Yes. Our job here is done. I have the money in my purse, and we can go home."

"Awww, I was hoping to see the rest of the house," I pouted.

"Did you forget you have a guest waiting for you?"

"Oh! You're right! Let's hurry home," I started running ahead until mother yelled and I returned to her side to take a more conservative pace on our journey home.

***

As soon as we arrived back at our little seasonal home, I changed into my favorite blue dress, tied a ribbon in my hair and dabbed some of mother's perfume on my wrists and neck. Normando would expect me to arrive looking presentable for a cup of his finest tea.

I found his wagon out by a grouping of four palm trees, nestled in their shade. A gentle knock and the door opened to reveal Normando's wide grin as he extended his arm towards the table, inviting me to take a seat.

"Greetings, my fine lady," he welcomed me with his usual flair. He pulled out a chair, and I sat down as daintily I could; pretending I was a princess at a royal event…until I giggled.

"Something amuses you?" Normando asked with a grin.

"I'm not nearly as lady-like as I pretend to be when I'm here with you," I admitted.

Normando sat down, and his expression turned serious. "You know you never have to pretend with me, my dear."

"Oh, but I like to! It's fun—like a game," I assured him.

"Alright. But, just remember, it is always best to be yourself. Never put on a show just to please people."

"But, Normando, isn't that what we do? Isn't that what the circus does? You do it all the time!"

"Oh, no, child," he corrected me with a wagging finger and scrunched-up eyebrows. "Normando is Normando because it pleases…Normando!"

I laughed and he smiled, but we both knew the importance of what he was saying.

"It's perfectly fine to do things that bring smiles to people's faces, to bring happiness to the world. But, you must be doing those things that you love, that bring happiness to you. I enjoy all the time and effort it takes to be the showman that I am. Your mother enjoys all the work she puts into sewing and crafting fancy costumes. And because we love what we do, others love what we do as well."

He turned his attention to a tea pot resting in a cozy, keeping warm; and brought it to the table.

"Today we have a delightful Darjeeling tea," he introduced the tea as he poured it. "Direct from India, this tea has a musky spiciness with a floral aroma. It is sometimes referred to as the champagne of teas."

"Ooooh. Fancy!"

Normando gave me a wink, and we sat and sipped tea and discussed my vivid imagination regarding Mrs. Frost and her parties. We heard a horse neighing in the distance, and our conversation turned to the animals and the performances in the circus.

"I wish I could have seen my father as the lion tamer," I lamented. "I bet he was wonderful."

"Oh, indeed he was!" exclaimed Normando. "No one has ever loved an animal like your father loved those lions. Did I ever tell you the story about the incident in South Carolina?"

"No, I don't believe so!"

Normando pulled his chair closer to the table. "We were in a quaint little town. I don't remember the name, but it had one of the tidiest town squares I'd ever seen. Peach of a place. Well, before an afternoon show one day, your father heard the lions making noise outside the tent; sounding distressed. He stepped out and saw some hoodlums poking sticks into the cages and throwing rocks."

"How did they even get that close?"

"Well, this was before your father implemented all his safety measures. There weren't even crewmen around because they had stepped away to smoke or something! Anyway, your father told those boys to move along, but they wouldn't do it. Next thing you know, he goes after them with the bullwhip! Hits one of them across the face, and draws blood!"

"No! Really?" My eyes must've been as big as the saucers that our tea cups sat on.

"Yes! Turned out it was the mayor's son." Normando got a disgusted look on his face. "Needless to say, we were told to pack up and leave right away."

"I bet Mr. Lewis was furious."

"You would have thought so, but no! He told your father he would've paid money to see the look on those boys' faces when he cracked that whip," Normando said with a guffaw.

We had just finished our tea when his cuckoo clock struck the hour, and I knew it was time for me to go home. Just as I was about to leave, I noticed a pale yellow feather on the floor.

"Normando, you've lost a feather!"

"I have? I didn't know I had feathers!" he teased.

"No, silly, not you. One of your costumes, I mean! Look here," I showed him the feather up close.

"Hmmm. I don't recall what that could possibly be from."

"It's lovely," I commented, turning it over in my hand.

"Why don't you keep it. A token to remember our tea together."

"Really?"

"Yes, I insist."

"Why I practically have a collection now!"

"You do? You're collecting feathers?"

I blushed and told him how Albert had given me a feather when we first arrived here at the fairgrounds.

"Oh, I see. Well, you need three or more to make a collection official; so I'll be on the lookout for any collecting-worthy specimens."

I gave Normando a hug and ran off to show mother my prize.

***

A few days later, all the circus folk were abuzz with the news. Mrs. Frost had hired a few of the smaller acts to perform at her next social gathering. She was throwing a holiday party to raise money to build a children's wing at the local hospital, and had decided circus acts would remind people of their childhood and motivate them to give.

Arman and Cryus would perform with snakes and sword-swallowing in the front yard as guests entered. The Martinelli family would perform acrobatics in the backyard during cocktails, and Albert and Pricha would be the grand finale during dessert. Normando was credited with making the suggestion to Mrs. Frost, and she hired him to emcee the entire shindig.

"How did Normando manage to meet Mrs. Frost?" I asked mother, bursting with curiosity.

"Well," she looked around and then whispered, "they are second cousins, and have stayed in touch over the years. This party is the reason Normando is here. And the reason she had me make that dress."

I felt like I had been let in on an international secret of national security. No one besides mother, and now myself, knew any of this. I was now part of an elite group of secret-keepers. But, why would this be such a secret? Now, my curiosity set in, and I yearned to ask mother more.

"Mother…"

"You need to get these costumes to the Martinelli girls right away. If they've grown too much, I'll have a lot of alterations to do. Go on, now."

I did as I was told, and ran off with my delivery for mother. Along the way, Normando came walking alongside me.

"I suppose you've heard about the party."

"Yes, I…" I almost let out my knowledge of the secret, but decided it best to keep quiet. "I heard from mother!"

"Well, I was thinking…after hearing your fanciful renditions of Mrs. Frost's parties, maybe it would be good for you to see for yourself. Better to have solid knowledge of the facts than to rely on assumptions and imagination."

"How would I go about seeing for myself? I'm not in any of the acts."

"Well, you could be, just this once. I could benefit from an assistant."

I stopped in my tracks, frozen with disbelief.

"Do you mean it? Are you just teasing?" I questioned.

"I mean it! You can fetch me food and drinks between performances, and help me touch-up my makeup. You'll need your own costume, though. Something glittery…and maybe with feathers."

"Oh! Oh!" I jumped up and down with excitement. "I'll do it! And, I'll have mother whip me up something!"

I looked down at the costumes in my hands. "But, first I must get these to the girls." I took off running, but remembered my manners and ran back to give Normando a hug and tell him thank you before running off again.

***

The night of the party, I was a basket of nerves. Not once had I been in costume, except as an infant for a nativity scene—a girl baby Jesus! It wasn't as if I had any lines to say or stunts to perform. My only duties were to assist Normando with his makeup and fetch him any supplies he may need. Nothing difficult. I'd been taking orders and running errands all my life! But, to be there—at a social gathering of the county elite—weighed me down and twisted my stomach into knots like I never thought possible. All those people...looking at me.

"I can't do it!" I yelled at mother as she finished tightening the knot in the thread holding on a button.

"Yes, you can. Now, stand up straight and let me get a look."

"No, I can't. They'll all be looking at me."

"Actually, they won't. They'll be looking at Normando. He captures the attention of everyone within a six-mile radius," she said with a grin. Mother turned me around to face a mirror. Standing before me was a teenage girl with her long hair twisted up on her head and held in place by a gold comb with white feathers; wearing a dress knee-high in front and ankle-length in the back of white with red and gold trimmings, gold buttons, and fringe. Her face was blushing with rouge and red-coated lips. Her feet adorned in sequined white slippers. Who was this girl? Oh, that's right...it was me.

To get to the party, I rode beside father in the truck, and noticed he kept glancing over at me and frowning.

"You don't like it?" I finally asked him.

"Your mother did an excellent job. The costume is beautiful."

"But, you don't like it."
Father sighed. "I'm not too keen on you being so...dolled-up," he admitted.

"I'm fourteen years old. Some of the show girls are only two years older."

"I know, I know. But, they aren't my daughter." He dropped me off around the side of the Frost house where Normando had parked his wagon.

"Break a leg!" father called out before driving off, leaving me standing alone on a sidewalk in the fading sunlight of dusk, in my red and white sequins and feathers…with butterflies in my stomach.

Within minutes, Normando was escorting me into the Frost home to show me where he would be introducing the acts, and where we would go to escape the crowd when needed.

I stepped through the side door; the one used by maids, cooks and servers, and followed Normando down a narrow hall, past the kitchen entrance, and into a large room aglow with lights from the tallest Christmas tree I had ever seen. It had to have been ten feet tall, and it glittered more than Normando and I put together. A large mahogany dining table sat in the middle of the room, covered with bowls and platters of enticing food, candles and flowers, and shimmering little Christmas ornaments.

I could hear the musicians warming-up and tuning their instruments in the back courtyard. Servers rushed around setting out dishes; maids scurried about putting finishing touches on flower arrangements and lighting candles; pots and pans still clattered in the kitchen. The sights, sounds and scents were almost overwhelming, and Normando had to snap his fingers to regain my attention.

"So sorry," I muttered.

"It's alright. I forget you've never seen such things. Let's go to the front where we'll begin, and walk through the events of the evening."

***

Arman and Cyrus, dressed in puffy white linen pants and turbans with large medallions in the center, mesmerized guests entering the party with boa constrictors and swords that disappeared into their mouths and reappeared without causing any harm.

Normando greeted people in the entry, and I stood nearby awaiting his command and offering a small, polite nod as they passed me by.

As I expected, the Martinelli's wowed the crowd that gathered in the back yard to watch them jump, flip, and stand on each other's shoulders in beautiful formations. But, the showstopper was certainly Albert performing somersaults atop Pricha's back while the guests sipped on hot chocolate and nibbled on red velvet cake.

I was allowed a few tastings during the evening, with the exception of anything containing alcohol. Normando had enough of that for both of us. He was acting even more flamboyant than usual when the party came to an end; speaking loudly and laughing heartily. Everyone just assumed it was part of his act; so no one seemed concerned.

As I made my way toward the side door to leave, Mrs. Frost called to me.

"Aren't you Helen's girl?"

"Yes, ma'am."

"Sadie," she called to one of her cooks. "Send a tray of food with…what's your name, dear?"

"Ruth, ma'am."

"A lovely name for a lovely girl. Sadie, make sure Ruth gets an armload to take with her."

And indeed she did. Father had to help me carry the stacks of glazed ham, rolls, stuffed olives, cookies and even a whole pie. We ate from our stash of party food for three days.

The next day, mother asked if she could turn my costume into something for one of the show girls. I hesitated to give it up, but I knew deep down that I'd never wear it again. Would have been a shame to let it go to waste. So, I pulled out one feather, a red one, and added it to my collection—three made it official—and gave the costume to mother. I still didn't know what I would do with my life in the circus, but I knew what I wouldn't do: perform.

***

CHAPTER SIX

"**You really never** performed?" I asked Ruth, a bit skeptical of her declaration.

"Never. It didn't appeal to me—the thought of all those people looking at me, watching me. No, sir." She shook her head as if to reinforce her point.

"More like your mother, then…a behind-the-scenes type person."

"Well, truth be told, my mother would have probably loved performing. She simply didn't have a skill or talent that was suitable for demonstrating in a circus show. My father, however, was never much into the performance."

"But, he was the lion tamer at one time."

"Yes, but his goal was to display the majesty of the lions he so loved. He was in awe of them, and longed to share that feeling with the crowd. He drew the audience's attention to the animals, not himself."

"Ahhh, I get it, now. No wonder he was at peace with his new position as manager. He was never really a performer to begin with."

"Exactly," Ruth affirmed before taking a sip of her now lukewarm tea.

"O.k., so I have a few questions."

"Alright. Go ahead."

"So far you've mentioned the lion tamer, elephant trainers, acrobats, show girls, snake charmers and a ringmaster. Seems to me some acts are missing."

"We were a family, as I said; but even families have groups within themselves that are closer than others. My portion, if you will, of the circus family was the group I've told you about." As she spoke she picked up the tea pot and poured a little to heat up her cup. "We also had trapeze artists, a tattooed man who did some sort of sideshow that I was too scared to see; other acts that any circus would have."

"I see. I was just curious."

"I could try to include some of them, if you like. My memory is pretty sharp—I can recall a few stories."

"I want you to share what you feel like sharing," I assured her.

"Another reason I'm glad I chose you," Ruth told me with a smile and a pat on my knee.

"I have to say, though; it might help the story with readers if there were clowns. Everyone loves clowns..."

"Not I! And not every circus story needs clowns. In fact, this isn't entirely a circus story. No. No clowns," she demanded, red-faced and wide-eyed.

"Alright, alright. No clowns! You obviously don't like them."

Ruth composed herself, and began to speak in her normal tone, "The men who performed as clowns were always creepy to me. In their makeup, I found them to be scary, and as themselves they were cantankerous drunks. So, you're correct in your assumption that I do not like them. Not that all clowns are that way, but you know…that was my experience. I'd prefer to leave them out."

"Agreed," I nodded my approval. "The tattooed man might be cool, though," I said with a wink and flashed my favorite ink that resides on my upper left arm.

"Oh, a feather!" Ruth exclaimed. "Now, what does it say? I don't have my glasses."

"It says, 'By words the mind is winged.' It's a quote from Aristophanes. And the feather is actually a quill pen."

She eyed my arm closely and smiled. "Lovely. Just lovely."

***

I hopped on Bonnie and went to put in a couple of hours at the paper. Katz caught me as I walked through the door, and waved me toward his office.

"Close the door." He said as he as he took off his brown rimmed reading glasses and sat them neatly on his desk.

I hated when he said that—made me feel like when I was a kid and got called into the principal's office.

"What's up?" I asked, trying to seem relaxed.

"I just discovered something interesting. Thought you should know about it."

I sat down. "O.k."

"Last month, someone ordered a bunch of archived articles from your former employer—ya know, the big city paper with their heads up their…"

"Yeah, yeah, I know. So?"

"So, the articles were all written by you. And, I bet you'll never guess the subject matter."

I stood up. "You think someone's investigating again? Or another suit is being filed?"

"Possibly. I have a contact over there who thought it was information worth sharing. They obviously think something's up."

I sat back down and began tapping my fingers on the arms of his office chair. The last thing I wanted was this mess from my past brought back to life.

"Maybe it's nothing. Some college kid doing some research for an essay or whatever," I suggested.

"Yeah, right," Katz said with sarcasm. "I'm sure that's it. Look, you should prepare yourself for the possibility that all that could resurface."

He was right. Preparation would be good. But, I preferred denial, ignoring and hiding.

"Think I'll skip writing on Ruth's story today. I already gave you my piece for tomorrow's edition."

"Read it this morning. Good stuff. Why don't you get outta here. You look like you could use a stiff drink."

"That's exactly what I'm going to get," I said as I walked out of his office and straight for Bonnie. She took me to 9th Bar for a double espresso. Most guys I know turn to beer in stressful or emotional situations. Me? I turn to coffee. I ordered three— one to drink there and two to take home.

That's the downside to riding a motorcycle, though—no cup holders. I held one of those fast food join drink carriers with my two espressos in one hand and steered Bonnie with the other. Not my best idea, but we made it home in one piece.

I dropped my backpack by the door, and set my coffee in the kitchen on the yellowed Formica countertop. Rubbing the back of my neck with one hand, and waving the other hand about like an Italian telling a really good story; I paced the floor and contemplated the various scenarios that could possibly explain someone gathering all my articles. My lips moved to the words spoken in my mind. If anyone had spied on me through the window, they would have thought I'd lost my marbles.

I decided I could always excuse my behavior as a coffee-high, and no one would give it a second thought. But, my pacing around the room, talking to myself was not the issue. I needed to learn more about the person that ordered those archives and why they wanted them.

Grabbing one of my extra espressos, I took out my phone and scrolled through my contacts; reluctantly pressing the green button to call an old friend from my past.

"Yeah," answered the voice on the line.

"Uh, Ben?"

"That's me. Who's this?"

"It's Michael...the reporter..."

"Mike! Man, it's been a long time. You kinda disappeared after everything."

"Yeah, I know. Look, I found out something today, and I, um...I think you should either be informed about what's happened; or if you already know, you should tell me what's going on."

***

Ben had no information to share, but he promised to let me know if he heard anything. It wasn't much relief, but it was enough that I could shift my focus to Ruth's story and get some writing done.

I pressed play on the recorder and listened again as she told me about Albert's father and the scene that played out in front of everyone. My own father had been an alcoholic, and I had suffered humiliation at his hands more than once. By the time he sobered up, the damage was done—both to his liver and to our relationship. I had empathy for Albert. That kind of abuse and rejection weighs heavily on a kid.

The story Ruth told of her tea with Normando was more significant than she may have realized. His advice was right-on, and something she obviously took to heart in how she lived her life. Normando wasn't acting; he was being himself, and was happy with the version of himself he had created. Ruth was certainly comfortable in her own skin, and didn't seem to need anyone's approval. She had her own ideas about who she was and what she wanted to do even as a young girl.

It occurred to me there were definite life-lessons to be gleaned from her story, and that maybe this was the angle to use in writing her story—How to Live Your Life: Lessons from the Lion Tamer's Daughter.

I jotted down the first two that came to mind.

1. Be yourself
2. Do what you love

Nothing profound, but definitely sound advice. The recording came to the part of the story where Ruth accompanied Normando to the party. How I wished she had shown me a picture of herself in that costume! I'd have to ask her if she had one. Maybe she had just forgotten. What was I thinking? Ruth didn't seem to forget anything!

Regardless, I was anxious to hear more, and found myself awaiting more of her story with more anticipation than ever…especially if she included the tattooed man.

***

"You asked for a story about some of the other people in the circus," Ruth began as she set her tea cup down and picked up a stack of pictures that had been placed on the bed.

"Did you think of something? A story to add?" I asked, excited to hear about a new character.

"I did! I came across this picture." She handed me a black and white photo of a thin man with a handlebar moustache, wearing an undershirt with dress pants and holding a little girl about three or four years of age.

"Who's this?"

"Look closely," she instructed.

Upon closer examination, I realized the man's arms were covered in tattoos.

"The tattooed man!" I exclaimed, thrilled that she had found this photo, and hopeful there was a story to go with it.

"His name was McGhee. That was probably his last name, but that's all anyone called him so that's all I know about him. I'm the child in his arms."

"You are? So he was in your 'inner circle'?"

"Not exactly. He mostly socialized with the crew and other performers that didn't have families. But, he is very important, and I can't believe I had almost completely forgotten him."

"Tell me more," I said as I pressed the button to record.

"When I was around two years old, probably a year before that picture was taken, mother would let me toddle around outside while she sat under a shade tree and worked on embroidery. One day, I toddled off a little further than usual and stepped on a hornet's nest. At first they just flew up and buzzed all around, but then they began to sting. I remember the sound of their buzzing and crying, and trying to run to my mother only to stumble to the ground.

Suddenly, arms wrapped around me and I was swept away so quickly a breeze hit my face as if I was flying through the air. McGhee had grabbed me and carried me to safety in a nearby building. He was stung multiple times during that rescue, and swelled up so bad he couldn't perform for a week. Tattoos aren't nearly as impressive with giant red whelps covering them. The pirate ship tattoo that covered his back looked as if it had been in battle…and lost," she said with a chuckle.

"Wow. He probably saved your life."

"I'm sure he did. I'm grateful to have come across the picture so that I could share the memory of heroism."

"I appreciate the story very much. But, I guess we need to stay on track with our timeline," I suggested, disappointed that this story was probably too far back to include in whatever it was I was going to write.

"You're right. Shall we continue with December 1941?"

"Yes, we shall."

CHAPTER SEVEN

It was the day after the party and I had just handed over my costume to mother so she could turn it into something for someone else, and felt terribly sad over it. I kept to myself most of the day, until later that afternoon.

Being Sunday, no one was working; so a group of women gathered in one of the exhibition halls of the fairgrounds to quilt and listen to the radio. I decided to join them—only to hear the radio, not to quilt. It started out as any other radio program, but was soon interrupted by a news bulletin. I quit paying attention once I heard that news flash. That is, until I heard the gasps and saw the faces of the women as they dropped their needles and reacted in horror. My gaze turned to my mother for an explanation. She just looked at me with this great sadness, like I had never seen before; a look of doom.

The news was about the attack on Pearl Harbor. Once I caught on to what was being said, I was terrified. If they could attack there, they could attack anywhere. If they were targeting ports and shorelines, we were dangerously close to those targets. My imagination ran away with me and when a truck started its engine outside; I was sure it was a plane, and ducked under a table.

For the rest of the day, people stayed near radios—working on trucks, cooking supper, mending clothes. Even the younger children played quietly with their marbles and such; as if they knew it was solemn time and that adults needed to hear every word of news.

That night, mother gave me some hot tea before bed. Knowing I would be too anxious to sleep, she had gone to Normando for some herbal tea that would help me rest. It must have worked because I slept soundly, and don't remember having any nightmares or waking during the night.

The following day we gathered again to hear President Roosevelt deliver his speech, requesting congress to declare war. My father stood there with a stone face of resolve. I believe he had made up his mind then and there to serve any way he could. Mother took one look at him, and then hung her head in grief. She wouldn't fight him or attempt to persuade him. She knew that he would get us settled somehow, and then go off to fight. There'd be no stopping him.

After a few days of whispered discussions, circulated gossip, and 'round-the-radio gatherings; the circus family was called to an official meeting in the largest exhibition hall. Mr. Lewis and my father were to address everyone, and this got us all nervous. A few people had suggested we go back on the road to perform; maybe join the USO to boost the morale of our soldiers. It wasn't even plausible, but the idea gave some comfort to those of us fond of wishful thinking.

Everyone assembled as requested, and father cleared his throat loudly to get our attention. "Thank you for coming together. I know you all have other things to do, so we will make this brief. First off, Mr. Lewis has some things to share."

Mr. Lewis quietly and deliberately stepped forward, looking over the entire group before he began to speak. "I have been informed that the Volusia county fairgrounds can no longer be our winter home."

People gasped, shouted "what?"—a few immediately began to cry.

"Quiet down, people. The fairgrounds are to be turned into a war production plant. They've given us 'til the new year, but then we…including our animals…must vacate this property."

"Where are we gonna go?" shouted a crewman from the back of the hall.

Mr. Lewis hung his head, took out a handkerchief and blew his nose. Father stepped up beside him.

"We are finalizing some arrangements for the animals, but as for everyone else…you must figure things out for yourself. The circus is disbanding."

More gasps, yells and tears. Father banged on a table to restore order.

"We have too many able-bodied men, willing to enlist, willing to fight. We can't continue to perform as if nothing is going on. I'm taking a group of men to the enlistment center the first week of January. I've made arrangements for my wife and daughter to live with family…"

After those words, I heard nothing else. This was the first mention of any such plans in my presence. No one had told me father was leaving. No one had told me I was leaving my circus family to live with "family" I didn't know. Every sound in that hall became a muddled echo that reverberated through my head—nonsense noise that overwhelmed me.

I caught a glimpse of Albert running out the door, towards the elephant barn. I followed after him. He ran nonstop to the barn at a pace I couldn't match. By the time I got there, Albert was leaning against Pricha, who stopped snacking on hay long enough to rub her trunk along the top of Albert's head as if she was comforting him. Albert just stood there, crying and wiping his eyes with his shirt sleeve.

"Albert?' I whispered as I took a few tentative steps towards him and Pricha. Albert looked my way, but quickly turned back towards Pricha and buried his face against her. I took a few more steps. "Albert, what're we gonna do?"

He turned his head and looked at me with anger. "I don't know! How am I supposed to know what we're gonna do? We're bein' kicked out, and left alone to do whatever! We ain't got no family to go to like you do!"

I broke down into heavy sobs and collapsed to my knees on the hay-covered dirt floor of the barn. My hair fell over my face so I didn't notice when Albert ran towards me. The next thing I knew was he had his arms wrapped around me, and we were sitting in the dirt; turning it into mud with our tears.

***

The next day, Albert invited me to join him to walk Pricha to a nearby pond. Hank, one of the elephant trainers, was walking Ginger, an older female, to the pond as well; so mother felt it safe enough for me to go.

Florida doesn't have much in the way of winter weather, but it was definitely cooler—cool enough for my new blue cardigan sweater mother had gotten by trading some mending of dresses and suit jackets for a family in town. It had three buttons down the front and a pocket on each side; just the right size to hold a few apple slices.

"Here," I handed Albert an apple slice, and he fed it to Pricha. I laughed.

"That was meant for you, silly!"

"I know, but if I don't share, Pricha will steal it."

I handed him another slice, and he ate it himself. Pricha reached her trunk over as if asking for more. I obliged.

"Mr. Lewis found a place for her," Albert's eyes looked down at the ground as his voice grew quiet.

"Where?"

"Another circus winters in Sarasota. They're interested in her…in our act."

"Your act?" I knew what he meant. That he and Pricha would be leaving to join another circus. That our time together would end soon. That it was all really coming to an end.

"I don't want to be without her. So, if they'll take us, we're going…together. My mother and sisters want to go live with cousins and get regular jobs. Not me. I'm a performer. And Pricha and I are partners. I can't leave her now." He reached in my pocket for another apple slice and fed it to Pricha.

It felt as though my whole world was crumbling down around me. "I hate this. I mean, I'm happy you get to stay with Pricha. I just hate…"

"All the separation. Everyone going different directions."

"Yeah." I sniffled as I wiped tears from my cheeks with my hand.

Albert took my hand and squeezed it. My heart skipped two beats…maybe three. The rest of the day we walked around together and talked; sometimes holding hands. With the shock of the previous day's announcement, everyone had been given the opportunity to take the day to make arrangements for work and places to live. Even though my arrangements were made for me, without my consent, I was given the day off from helping with the little ones—and I took full advantage.

Eventually, Albert and I wandered to a grouping of palm trees where we found Normando sitting on a stool that looked too small and precarious for him to trust with his full weight; leaning towards a canvas on an easel with a paintbrush in his hand.

"I didn't know you painted!" I remarked.

"I don't really, dear. I mean, I'm not a painter, per se. It's just something I like to do to relax," he explained with all the grandiose gestures of a ringmaster.

"Looks good to me," Albert complimented, stepping closer to get a better look.

"Thank you, kind sir. So, what brings you two out this far? Don't you have chores to do or something?"

"Not today. Everyone is panicked, trying to figure out where to go and what to do. Thankfully, Mr. Lewis had already made some calls for me and Pricha."

"Oh, that's good to hear. And you, Ruth?" Normando asked—I had assumed he already knew.

"Mother and I are to go live with her sister and brother-in-law. I guess I have a cousin."

"That sounds promising!" Normando turned back to his painting.

"What about you?" I asked, and my voice cracked as I fought back more tears.

"Oh, I don't know. I'll call around and find something to do. For now, I'm going to paint and visit my cousin in town for tea."

"I know who your cousin is," I boasted.

Normando faced me. "So, you're in on the secret."

"What secret?" Albert asked.

"Normando has a famous cousin is all," I teased. "Correction! My cousin has a famous cousin—the great Normando!" He spoke his name with all the fervor of an opening night performance, with one arm raised over his head and the other on his hip. When he stood, his stool fell over backwards and nearly knocked over his easel; but he held his pose like a gymnast sticks a landing. For a split second, I thought I saw a tear down run his cheek. But, I must've been mistaken because his eyeliner and rouge were still perfect.

***

Christmas Eve, and there was only a smidge of excitement. Not only was our deadline for leaving drawing near, but our fathers and brothers would soon be heading out to war, and our country had been thrown into extraordinary circumstances. Few people in town used decorative lights. Those who did only had them lit an hour each night. They didn't even have a parade—a yearly tradition that I sorely missed. It just didn't feel like Christmas. No one seemed to feel like celebrating.

Sugar and butter were rationed, which made holiday baking difficult. With rubber and metal in demand for the war effort, traditional toys were hard to find. Most toy makers had switched to using materials that were plentiful in supply. I had gone with my mother and some of her friends to shop for the younger children. The boys would be getting wooden jeeps and cardboard "Bild-a-Sets." A few fortunate little girls would receive Betsey Wetsy dolls, but most would get paper doll sets and a homemade baby-doll pieced together from fabric scraps.

Not that Christmas was all about food and gifts, but as children, those are the things you cherish and remember. How I wished it was a normal holiday with all the sweets and presents a child could want. War was bad enough on any ol' day, but war at Christmas was downright miserable.

The weather was just a tad cool with drizzly rain. Albert was spending lots of time outdoors without a coat; saying he was preparing himself for the cold weather up north when he traveled with his new circus. I got mad at him. First, for being foolish enough to risk getting sick; and then for going to a new circus. I was going to miss him, and I was jealous that he would get to continue the life—the only life I had ever known. It made me furious.

"What're you all huffy about?" he asked me, after I had gone silent and sullen.

"You shouldn't be out here without a coat. You're gonna get pneumonia."

"Nah, I'm fine. Besides, it'll be a heck of a lot colder where I'm headin'. Gotta prepare myself."

"Hmph," I replied, and rolled my eyes.

"There you go again…getting' huffy."

I stopped and crossed my eyes and looked away from him so he couldn't see me fight back my tears.

He walked closer to me, put his arm around my shoulders and kissed my cheek!

"It's sweet that you're worried about me. I promise I'll be fine."

I turned to look at him and caught my breath. We had never been this close before.

"It's not just that. You're going off with another circus. I'm going to live with family I've never met. We…we may never see each other again."

"Nonsense, Ruthie. This war will be over soon, and we'll all get back together. You'll see. Besides, I can write you and tell you all about the places Pricha and I go. It'll be like I'm right there with you."

"Now who's talkin' nonsense?"

He smiled great big, gave me a wink, and began walking towards the living quarters he still shared with his mother and sisters.

"Going home already?" I asked, sounding terribly whiney.

"Gotta spend some time with the family. Only a couple days left before I leave. See ya tomorrow."

My heart sank. I wanted him back by my side, his arm around me, and his lips on my cheek. Better yet, on my lips!

"Ruthie!" my father called from behind me. "Your mother needs your help. Get home, and tell her I'll be there shortly."

"Yes, sir!" I ran towards our little house, and tried my best not to cry.

***

Mother had a way of taking my mind off my troubles—she kept me busy being her assistant as she finished dresses and dolls that would be gifts the following morning. We also had some baking to do, having saved-up our rationed sugar to make a chocolate pecan cake. Normando had supplied us with the pecans with the stipulation that he get to "partake of the cake, as well." Of course, we invited him to celebrate Christmas with us and partake of all the food we had to offer.

Once the cake was in the oven, I turned my attention to wrapping the present I had for Albert. My little bit of work caring for the younger children had earned me enough money to buy him a nice pair of gloves for that cold, northern weather. Mother had some scrap grey material, and using her artistic talents, cut two elephant silhouettes from it, and stitched one on each glove. She was an amazing, seamstress—my mother. I was so pleased that Albert's gloves were original and handcrafted. They were something he could cherish that would remind him of the skinny Clarke girl whom he gave a feather and a kiss on the cheek.

***

Christmas morning arrived, and despite the gloom of the war and weather; most everyone was cheerful. The youngest among us ran outside to show and share their new toys. Women were basting turkeys and peeling potatoes. Men were smoking pipes while playing checkers or a game of cards.

For a while, it all felt normal; as it should. I nervously held Albert's gift in my hands, and walked to the exhibition hall where Albert was watching a group of crewmen play cards. He noticed me walk in, and waved me over to him.

"A couple of these guys are good—real good. They got nerves of steel, I tell ya," he whispered. "Straight-faced and bluffin'. Wish I could do that."

"You can't keep a straight face?"

"Nah. Everything I'm thinkin' and feelin' shows right up here," he said, pointing to his eyes. "I give it all away."

I stood by him and watched for a moment before barely muttering, "Got ya something."

He looked shocked, and then embarrassed.

"It's ok. I wasn't expecting anything," I assured him. "Just wanted you to have something to remember me by."

We walked away from the game, and he took the box and tore off its newspaper wrapping. He glanced at me before opening the box, and then…

"They're…amazing."

"You really like them?" I asked, hoping he was genuine.

"Oh, yes. They're perfect for the winter weather, and the elephants…the stitching," he caressed the gloves and looked me in the eye. I could see tears forming.

"I'm glad you like them," I whispered.

Albert leaned in, and I closed my eyes. A gentle touch of his lips against mine lingered for two or three breaths. The sound of someone clearing their throat startled us, and our lips parted.

"Ruth, dear," said Normando, "time to help your mother prepare food. Best be going."

"Yes, um…I was just…um, I'll head that way now!"

I didn't even look at Albert before I took off running toward home. Not a drop of that cool, drizzly rain bothered me. I was warm—aglow with the radiant heat of young love and a first kiss.

***

Our Christmas Day feast spread across the table like a demonstration of prosperity in the midst of despair. No ham, and only two desserts; but plenty of everything else: turkey, dressing, mashed potatoes, green beans, asparagus and cranberry sauce. It was more like a Thanksgiving meal, but we didn't mind. We certainly had a lot to be thankful for. While we hated the idea of Father leaving to fight in a war; at least Mother and I had a place to go and family to live with. I was particularly thankful for the stationary set I had received; as I intended to use every last bit of it writing to Albert.

Normando sat at the table with his spectacular posture and air of royalty, wearing a red silk dress coat trimmed in gold; his cheeks rosy with blush and his eyeliner perfect. He looked so regal; it was as if an Ambassador or prestigious foreign ruler had come to be our holiday guest.

We took our time, enjoyed each bite, engaged in conversation. Though no one spoke of it, we all knew this would be our last gathering; at least for a long while. This day was for celebrating and embracing what made us family—circus family. Tomorrow would be a different day with no celebration. Tomorrow's embracing would involve tearful goodbyes. And in the midst of joyous recalling of our fondest circus memories; who would want to think about something as gloomy as tomorrow?

***

Alas, tomorrow arrived. Donald and Hank led the elephants out of the barn, through the giant wood gates that stood at the fairground entrance, and to the train tracks to board a freight train heading north. It was heart-breaking to see those majestic creatures evicted from their winter home.

Albert walked alongside Pricha, reassuring her as they went along. "It's alright, girl. You get a car all to yourself! I'll be waiting for you at the end of the trip, and we'll get to rehearsing right away."

He talked to her and pet her face until she reached the ramp to enter the train car. Without hesitation, Pricha walked inside and remained calm as they wrapped the chain around her leg. Albert's motivational speech must have worked because we all had feared Pricha would panic and struggle. Instead, she stood perfectly still and took a slice of apple from Albert's hand before they closed the door.

A cool breeze carrying droplets of rain hit my face and stung my eyes. The scarf I had tied around my head fell to my shoulders, and I struggled getting it back in place over my head and surrounding my face.

"Here, let me help," offered Albert, pulling my scarf tight around my face before leaning in for a quick kiss.

"Albert, not here—no now! My father is just over there."

"They're not looking," he said with a wink. "Gotcha somethin'."

He handed me a Prince Albert can, bright red tin with a portrait of the man himself standing erect in black and white and the words "crimp cut long burning pipe and cigarette tobacco" printed underneath.

"Tobacco?" I gave him a curious look.

"Look inside, silly."

The can opened to reveal a small collection of feathers; some brown and black, others an auburn color, and one that was a beautiful blue.

"Oh, Albert, they're lovely!"

"I've been collecting them here and there. That one is from a Blue Jay, I think. And, I figured the can would remind you of me. Ya know, so you don't forget."

"Forgetting you is utterly impossible."

We held hands and walked to the exhibition hall where everyone was gathering to say their goodbyes.

***

The group of men that had enlisted included my father, all the crewmen including William who was no longer considered the "new guy," Kristoff the lion tamer, Arman and Cyrus. Most of them would be staying in a boarding house in town until they got their orders; a few of the crewmen had already gotten their orders and were taking the train the next day.

Mother and I were taking an afternoon train to begin our journey to Fort Lauderdale. Everyone was chatting, promising to write, exchanging recipes and addresses; and basically acting as though we'd be together again in a few months— like a long vacation. Somehow I knew it wouldn't work out that way. Mother had taught me history along with all my other subjects up until I turned twelve. My education had included stories of American wars, our heroes and unfortunately our losses. Part of me was mad that they put on brave faces without giving this day the solemnness it deserved. But, deep inside, I realized that weeping and carrying-on would do no good. This was the better way.

"Almost time to head out!" father shouted over the crowd. The men all gave him a nod and gave final hugs and parting words to their loved ones and friends.

Father came to me and wrapped me in his arms. "I'll let you know where I am as soon as I get there. You write me every week, alright?"

"Yes, Sir. I'll write every day and just send it all each week."

"That's a lot of writing."

"There'll be a lot to say. I don't want you to go," I let out a few sobs and then fought to regain control.

"This is something I have to do. Not because I'm being forced to, but because it is the right thing to do. Our country needs us."

I nodded in agreement as best I could with my head still tucked into his arms and pressed against his chest.

"Ruthie, darling…is that a can of tobacco in your hand?"

I giggled and pulled myself out of his embrace. "No, father. It's a gift!" I opened it to show him the feathers, and he smiled and laughed heartily.

"A genius idea! The tin will keep the feathers safe and clean. And, they're pretty feathers, too—pretty like my girl."

The clock struck the hour, and father called out for the men to get to the truck. Mother gave him a long goodbye kiss that made me horribly uncomfortable so that I had to look away. Father drove with two men in the cab with him and the rest sitting in the bed of the truck. He honked and they all waved and blew kisses as they drove off down the dirt road.

I let my tears fall, but I didn't sob or wail like I wanted; just quiet tears in the chilly sprinkle of rain, watching my father head off to war.

CHAPTER EIGHT

"I can't even imagine," I whispered as I wiped a few stray tears with my sleeve.

"It was a very difficult time for me," Ruth admitted. "My father left for who-knew-where, and my mother and I were going off to live a strange life with strangers. At least, that was how I felt at the time. My whole family, men who were like brothers and uncles, were leaving; and I didn't know when or if I'd see them again."

"And Albert...just as you two had connected..."

"Care for more tea?" Ruth was attempting to redirect the conversation.

I didn't want to upset her, so I declined the tea and started packing my gear for the ride home.

"I should show you something," Ruth said, getting up from her chair and walking to a box that sat on top of a stack of other boxes. She took it down, opened it, pulled out a faded red Prince Albert can and handed it to me.

"You still have it! Are the feathers inside?" I asked, hopeful.

"They are. You can see for yourself."

I gently opened the tin and there inside were feathers of different sizes and colors. I didn't remove them or even touch them—simply admired them before closing the tin again.

"I added to my collection over the years, but those are my favorites."

"Obviously," I replied. "Any gift given to you by your first love in a tin with his name on it just has to be your favorite!"

Ruth grinned, and when she took the tin back into her hands, she held it against her heart.

***

A little while later, Bonnie drove me straight to work, against my will. You'd think that my having saved her from a dump and restoring her to near perfection, she'd be more grateful and take me to get espresso. But, no. We went to the newspaper to write an article and earn a paycheck.

"You got a call. The message is on your desk," Rebekka, one of our interns, told me.

"Thanks. I owe you a coffee."

"Careful. I'll take you up on that. But, none of that gas station stuff."

"I wouldn't dare!" I said winking.

Lying on my desk was a bright yellow sticky note with "Call Ben" scribbled on it. A knot formed in my stomach, but this was nothing to ignore. I checked my cell phone, and realized I had missed his call because my volume was down while I recorded Ruth. If he called my office, too... This couldn't be good.

"Yeah," he answered.

"Ben, it's Mike—returning your call."

"Hey, bud. We should meet up and talk."

He was trying his best to sound casual but I could sense the concern in his voice. "That sounds ominous."

"Looks like someone is digging into our case. I'd rather share what I know in person."

"Yeah, that's probably best. When and where?"

"I'll come your way if you buy the drinks."

"Deal. How about Pub 1933 at seven?"

"See ya there." He said before hanging up.

***

I sat in my chair, mind racing for a few moments. "Hey, boss," I called out to Katz, my editor. "Gotta sec?"

We went into his office and he closed the door before sitting on the edge of his desk.

"I still haven't made it over to your place to hear those recordings. Maybe next week. How's the ol' woman's interviews going? She rambling on or could it be something worth writing?"

"Ruth is actually an amazing storyteller. You'll love it. But, that's not what we need to talk about."

"Oh, right…the case. Find out anything?" he asked.

"I'm about to. Ben Maupin just called me and asked to meet tonight. He said there's definitely someone looking into our case."

He crossed his arms. I could see the wheels in his head moving. "Damn. I was hoping that archive thing was just a fluke."

"Me, too. I'm meeting Ben at seven. I'll fill you in tomorrow."

Katz eyebrows scrunched into a frown. "No, you won't! You'll call me right after your meeting! I want to know the details as soon as you get them. We might to need to get ahead of this thing."

"There may not be anything we can do! And whoever is investigating this may not even find anything actionable. We may be worried over nothing." I told him.

"We can't just sit back and wait to see what happens."

"I don't think we have much of a choice."

***

At seven-o-two I walked into Pub 1933, and found Ben sitting at the bar with half a bottle of beer.

"Got here early," he explained as he shook my hand, and I sat on the stool next to him.

"So, let's get right to it. What'd you find out?"
Ben took a slow sip of beer and hesitated before he
spoke. "Well…someone with internal affairs has
pulled case files; as has some intern from the district
attorney's office. I may have been promoted to
Lieutenant, but there is some information that only
Captains are privy to. So, I don't know exactly what
files were pulled or for what specific reason other
than to 'review.'"

"That could mean anything."

"What'll you have?" the bartender asked,
interrupting my train of thought.

"Don't drink, but thanks anyway." I said. The
bartender scowled at me and I looked at Ben. "We
can move to a booth or table."

Ben and I moved to a corner booth so we could
discuss things with a little privacy and so as not to
annoy the bartender with a non-drinker at his bar.

"Since when don't you drink?"

I shrugged. "I'm just not in the mood."

"You have to be in the mood?" Ben asked,
incredulously.

"I'm more a coffee guy. So, back to this
investigation that's going on. First, someone pulls
archives of the story from the paper; and now case
files are being gone through. Sounds like we may be
in for some retaliation."   I began fumbling with the
salt and pepper shakers just to keep my hands

occupied. The nerves were starting to go into overdrive.

"That's what I'm thinking. Man…I was hoping they'd let it be."
"So was I. So. Was. I."

***

I went straight home after my meeting with Ben, and pulled a bottle of soda and leftover pizza from the fridge. "I've got to start eating better," I whispered to myself, and threw the pizza in the trash. Nights spent eating fast food (or leftovers of fast food) while writing were taking the toll. I felt like crud.

Rummaging through the fridge again, I found half a head of lettuce that was surprisingly still good, and part of a cucumber and some shredded cheese. The last tablespoon of French dressing was just right; and I felt better having had a little salad, as sparse as it was.

Reluctantly, I walked to the old steam trunk I used for storage, and opened it up. The smell was a bit musty, and the files had been jostled the last time I moved. Papers were scattered and the folders were all out of order. I sighed heavily, and began pulling out papers that appeared to be what I was looking for—newspaper articles and court documents.

I grabbed onto one article, cut from a paper, and the headline dredged up memories I had hoped to forget.

Local Columnist Accuses Police of Corruption
Police Chief Denies Allegations

A loud banging on my front door caused me to jump and drop the newspaper clipping on the floor.

"It's me! Open the door!" Katz rumbled.

"Katz? What're you doing here?" I asked as I opened the door and he barged right inside.

"I brought wine!" He went straight to my kitchen and helped himself to two glasses, meant for iced tea, and began pouring. "It's a nice Chardonnay. You'll like it."

"Did it not occur you to, ya know maybe…call first? See if I was home? Check if I was willing to have company?"

"I'm your boss. You can't say no."

"Actually, I can."

He handed me a glass, and I took a sip.

"Tell me what you learned from Ben," he demanded as he plopped down onto my couch and took a drink of wine.

"Not much. Internal affairs and the D.A.'s office are pulling case files. We don't know why, and we still don't know who requested the article archives."

"So they're reopening the case."

"We don't know that either. Could be a general review or something."

"What are the odds of that?"

"Slim to none," I responded before taking another drink. Suddenly, wine seemed like a really good idea; if nothing else, to settle my stomach.

"I know you don't want to revisit all this, but you do know that you're in the clear, right? You and Ben did the right thing, and you got vindication."

"But, now we could be facing vengeance. That's what I'm afraid of." I said as I sat on the couch and rubbed my tired eyes.

"You think someone would try to alter evidence or something? What can they really do?"

"We're talking about corrupt people in places of authority. They can do whatever they please. Pour me some more wine."

Katz and I sat and talked for another hour before he sent for an Uber driver to take him home. I sat the empty wine bottle into the recycle bin and collapsed on my bed fully dressed. Tired as I was, sleep wouldn't come…not with all this on my mind.

***

The next morning, I showered and dressed in fifteen minutes so I'd have time to grab coffee on the way in to the office. Instead of a ponytail or "man-bun," I left my hair down; hanging past my shoulders, to air dry.

Bonnie took me to 9ᵗʰ Bar for a double espresso, and I was ever so grateful. I must have looked worn-out because Omar asked if I was feeling alright. I assured him it was just lack of sleep, and he poured me a cup to go, on the house.

About two hours was all I had at the office before I had to leave to meet with Ruth again. I finished my puff piece on an art exhibit at a local gallery, and ran it by Katz for approval.

"Geez," said Katz, rolling his eyes. "Your talent is such a waste writing this crap."

"Gee, thanks, boss," I said, sarcastically.

"I wish you'd let me put you on something else."

"I'd rather not."

Katz rolled his eyes again, and added a sigh for effect; tossing my newly written "crappy" article onto the far corner of his desk. "Whatever."

"I'm going to meet Ruth. All our talking last night, and we didn't listen to a single recording."

"Why don't you bring your recorder to my place Monday night. Margie will make dinner; I can drink my wine from a decent glass-"

"I get the picture. I'll check my schedule."

"What schedule? You have no life!" Katz yelled after me as I walked out his door.

He was right. Last night was the first time I had been even remotely social in a very long time, and that was only because of the recent troubling events. Maybe that was another reason I looked forward to my meetings with Ruth. I now considered her a friend; so maybe I had a life after all.

***

"So, Ruth, what comes next in your story?"

"I thought I'd tell you about life in Ft. Lauderdale, and my dear friend and cousin, Lizzie." The mention of her name put a warm smile on Ruth's face.

"The same Lizzie who owned this house?"

"The very same. I won't linger too long with this part because there's good stuff coming up."

I laughed heartily. "I have no doubt."

"I have something for you," she said, surprising me. She handed me a beautifully wrapped package with a blue bow on top.

"What's this?" I asked looking at the pretty paper.

"Just a small gift to show my appreciation. Go on, now...open it!"

Ripping the paper off and pulling the box open, I was pleased to find a porcelain coffee mug with the image of a vintage typewriter on it.

"This is awesome! Thank you."

"Turn it around," she instructed.

I turned the mug around in my hands, and on the other side it read: *By words, the mind is winged.*

"Perfect. I'll cherish it always." I leaned over and gave her a kiss on the cheek, and I swear she blushed.

"Now, then. Let's get started," she said as she pushed the record button herself.

CHAPTER NINE

It was seventy degrees with blue skies when Uncle Ed picked us up from the train station in his 1935 Ford truck, faded black with a touch of rust. He had a stern and worn-looking face, and walked with a limp. We helped him toss our luggage and boxes of belongings into the back, and then squeezed into the front—me in the middle.

Uncle Ed wasn't unpleasant, but he obviously wasn't thrilled with our being there. More than once he mentioned how he was "happy to help out in spite of the strain" we would be on his family; meaning he didn't need two more women-folk to provide for. Mother assured him we could work to earn our way if he could just provide us a room for a while. I was hoping Aunt Jane, my mother's sister, would be more...welcoming.

Their house wasn't much to look at; its only saving grace a screened-in porch on which to sit and enjoy the Florida sunshine without the bother of mosquitos. Uncle Ed worked at the Coca-Cola bottling company down the road, and proudly offered to serve us cold bottles of cola once we got our things inside.

"Lordy, Ed, who's this you brought to my house? It cain't be my sister and her baby? This girl is too big!" Aunt Jane said as she bounced down the porch steps and wrapped her arms around me, squeezing so I could hardly breathe.

She was four years older than my mother, but looked a decade older with her dark brown hair streaked with grey and wrinkles at the corners of her eyes and mouth. But, she smiled easily and spoke loudly with enthusiasm—much different than my mother. Uncle Ed actually relaxed around his wife, and when he smiled I was able to look past his initial gruffness and notice his baby blue eyes and strong chin; he was a handsome man.

Before I had a chance to turn back to the truck and get my suitcase, the screen door swung open and banged closed, and on the second step stood a girl about my age with strawberry blonde hair and freckles, grinning shyly.

"This here is Elizabeth—everyone calls her Lizzie. Come here, Lizzie, and say hello to your cousin!"

Lizzie walked like my mother, as if she was skittish and being forced to approach you. She stuck out her hand to shake mine, and then stared at her feet.

"You don't shake hands with family, girl! Give her a hug!" Uncle Ed instructed.

I leaned in and gave Lizzie a gentle hug, and she sighed and smiled; probably relieved I didn't squeeze like her momma.

Once we got our boxes stored on a shelf in their work shed in the backyard and our suitcases unpacked in the spare room that Uncle Ed's mother had lived in until she passed a few months back; we sat down to a feast of fried chicken, potatoes and gravy, and a lemon pie.

"You cook like Momma," my mother told her sister. "Best food I've eaten in ages."

"Aww, sis," Aunt Jane said, blushing while shaking her dish towel at momma in jest. "You shouldn't flatter me like that."

"No flattery—just honesty. You sit down and Ruth and me will do the dishes."

I was so tired and really didn't want to help with the dishes, but I had to admit the food was so delicious, I felt I owed Aunt Jane something in return.

"In the mornin' I'll make biscuits and tomato gravy," Aunt Jane informed us.

"What's tomato gravy?" I asked.

"You don't know what tomato gravy is?" Aunt Jane was obviously shocked.

"It's the best," Lizzie whispered as she stood next to me ready to dry the frying pan I had just washed.

"Helen, what have you been feeding this child? She hasn't had tomato gravy?" Aunt Jane asked of my mother, only half teasing.

"I'm not the cook you are," mother replied with a chuckle.

"Ruth, you come to the kitchen in the morning and I'll show you how to make tomato gravy. You and Lizzie can be my helpers."

That night I slept fitfully; waking with every dog howl, train whistle, and the occasional soft snore from mother. This was very unusual, but I had grown accustomed to sleeping in different environments when we traveled with the show. How I missed the comfort of our trailers and tents, the smell of campfires and exotic animals, the sounds of the crewmen getting rowdy as they played cards and the roars of the lions at night.

I woke for the third time just before the sun came up and decided to go on in the kitchen so I wouldn't fall asleep and miss Aunt Jane's lesson on tomato gravy. To my surprise, Lizzie was already in there, making coffee.

"Aren't you a little young for that stuff?" I asked. Lizzie laughed. "I'm only two years younger than you, and besides this ain't for me. It's for Momma. I was already awake anyhow."

"Me, too."

"Cain't sleep?"

I sighed heavily. "No."

"It's just 'cause it's a different place," Lizzie tried to reassure me.

"I've slept in lots of different places, traveling with the show."

"Oh, that's right! You were in the circus!"

"Well, not exactly. Anyway, I don't think it's being here that's the problem. It's not being there—with my circus family. You wouldn't understand."

Lizzie looked down at her feet, and I could tell I had hurt her feelings.

"I'm sorry, Lizzie. You all are family, of course. It's just…"

"It's alright. We don't know each other, and you've grown up with the people in the show, as you call it. Of course you miss them. No wonder you cain't sleep."

I smiled. Maybe Lizzie did understand. If she didn't then she was being awfully sweet.

***

Aunt Jane followed the scent of coffee into the kitchen, and joined us girls at the kitchen table. "Both you girls beat me to it this mornin'. Just let me get a few sips and we'll get started on the biscuits."

I had made biscuits before, but not using buttermilk, and not as efficiently as Aunt Jane and Lizzie. They had the mixing, rolling down to a science; and for cutting, they used an iced tea glass.

"Don't you have a biscuit cutter?" I asked Aunt Jane.

"Don't need somethin' else to take up space in this tiny kitchen. A glass works just fine; a circle's a circle."

I laughed, and took the glass from her hands so I could continue cutting biscuits while she fetched her canned tomatoes from the cellar.

First, she fried up some bacon. Once it was nice and crispy, the pulled the bacon and left the grease. Adding flour slowly, she whisked it into the grease. Then, she added the cans of tomatoes, using her wood spoon to break apart the tomatoes into smaller chunks. Finally, a little salt and pepper was added to complete the gravy.

By the time the biscuits were done, Mother and Uncle Ed had joined us in the kitchen and were sipping coffee while they waited to be served. I set a plate of hot biscuits and tomato gravy in front of my momma, and she smiled.

"You learn to cook like this from your Aunt Jane, and your daddy will never let me do the cooking again."

We all chuckled, but then a bit of somberness hit as we thought about where my father was and what he was soon to be doing.

"He's a good man, defending our country. If not for my bum leg, I'd be right beside him. Least I can do is house his wife and daughter 'til he returns—and he will return," Uncle Ed assured us.

"And he'll want some of this gravy when he does," added Aunt Jane. "I'll have you cookin' all your grandmother's recipes in no time."

Uncle Ed said a quick grace, and we all dug in to our delicious breakfast. I was beginning to think I just might like it here.

**

After New Year's, Lizzie was to return to school. I had hoped she'd be schooled at home like I was so we could do things together, and I told mother so.

"You could go to school, too," she suggested.

"No, I can't. I mean, I've done all my schooling."

"I'm sure there's a lot more you could learn."

"I'll borrow books from Lizzie and read a lot. I promise."

Mother laughed. "Alright, alright. I'm not going to make you go. It was just a suggestion."

I was so relieved. Reading was enjoyable, and I certainly liked to learn new things. But, school? I had never even been inside a school, and couldn't imagine it would be anything I'd like.

**

It was interesting how quickly a new routine formed. We are, after all, creatures of habit, as they say. I would help Aunt Jane in the kitchen preparing breakfast and packing lunches while Mother gathered eggs from the few chickens they kept, and pulled weeds. Uncle Ed went to work at the bottling company, Momma either went into town to deliver dress orders or went to work on her sewing machine, and Lizzie went to school. I'd take a nickel from the money I earned doing occasional babysitting or extra chores, and buy candy for myself and Lizzie before finishing my walk to meet her when school let out.

One day, I stood on the sidewalk waiting for Lizzie to appear amongst the throng of kids exiting the school in a hurry. I had bought us some rock candy, and anxiously awaited to hear everything she had learned. Though I still didn't want to go to school myself, I begged Lizzie to share all she could with me—especially from her science and history lessons.

As I waited, I caught a glimpse of a girl running from the playground and a group of boys following behind her, laughing. It wasn't just any girl; it was Lizzie. I dashed over to her in full sprint.

"Lizzie, what happened? Are you alright?"

She was crying and her face was beet red. "I'm fine. Let's just go."

I turned and saw the boys in their little huddle, still laughing.

"Were they picking on you? They're bullies, aren't they?"

"Ruth, let's just go…please."

I handed her the rock candy which brought a small grin to her face, and we headed for home.

That night, when everyone was asleep, I snuck to the work shed. The box of my father's belongings was on the top shelf, and I couldn't reach it from the ground. There were some old Coca-Cola crates stacked in a corner; so I drug them near the shelf, and stacked them to stand upon. Trying to maintain a grip on Uncle Ed's flashlight, I grabbed the box, but lost my balance on the crates and fell onto the dirt floor; scraping my leg on the soda crates.

After cleaning up my mess, I hobbled back to my room. It may not have been the most covert of operations, but my mission had been completed—I had what I needed.

***

The next day I met Lizzie at school, and demanded she take me to where those bullies hung out on the playground.

"But, why?" Lizzie whined. "They're nothin' but trouble. They tease, pull hair, steal money. Why would you want to go near them?"

"Just show me," I said sternly, patting the bag that hung off my shoulder.

We walked around the side of the building, towards the swings, and there were the boys gathered around the base of the slide. They looked a bit shocked to see us girls coming towards them, but they weren't the least bit afraid. Those boys just stepped towards us, side by side; forming a wall of intimidation.

"This is our turf. Ya'll need to go on home," said one of the boys, acting tough.

"Oh, so this is where the dumb bullies hand out? Well, I'm looking for a bunch of stupid boys that have nothing better to do than to pick on girls."
I couldn't believe that just came out of my mouth. I had never been so brave or so scared in all my life. The need to defend Lizzie overwhelmed me, and I kept going.

"What did you say? Sounds to me like you're askin' for it," another one of the boys chimed in.

"Askin' for what?"

"Askin' for trouble! Let's show 'em, boys!"
They made their move toward us, and I yanked my hand out of my bag and cracked my father's leather, lion whip. The snap was so loud it stopped the boys in their tracks.

"One more move, and I'll whip you all!" I cracked the whip again.

Those bullies just stood there dumbfounded; each waiting on one of the others to make the first move.

"I'm warning you all now. If you ever hassle Lizzie again, I'll take this whip to each of you. Ya hear me?"

They nodded and slowly backed away. I gave the whip one last crack, and they ran off. Not being skilled with the whip, I had managed to hit myself in the face and my cheek had a gash.

"You're bleeding!" Lizzie exclaimed.

"And it hurts so bad I want to cry...but don't tell them that. They're sufficiently scared. Let's just get home."

When we got home, Aunt Jane was terribly concerned about my cheek, and by then I had broke down in tears and told her about the scrape on my leg, too. Mother acted as though she was going to punish me, but then she smiled.

"You get your bravery from your father," she spoke quietly while she washed the cut on my face.

"I couldn't let Lizzie get picked on. It wasn't right."

"Ruthie the Defender...that's what your father would call you right now."

"I miss him."

"I do, too." She continued to clean my wounds, and we both wept silently wishing for his safe return.

***

A letter arrived on February 11th. It was our first correspondence from my father. It was postmarked from Britain, and I could barely contain myself not to rip it open standing right there at the mailbox. I yelled for my mother while I ran to the house, and burst through the door.

"We got a letter!"

"From your father?!" Now Mother was as excited as I was.

"Yes, ma'am! Look!"

My Dearest Helen and Ruthie,
We just arrived here in Britain, and will be moving on from here; where I'm not sure. They don't tell us much in advance. The British men are friendly enough, but they have been fighting for two years. They are tired, hungry and poor. We have arrived with full stomachs, plenty of rest, and money in our pockets. There is a certain amount of resentment, and honestly, it's understandable. Mostly, we all get along, though. I did break up a fight in which a couple of the British men hassled one of our youngest guys until he fought back. You know me; always looking out for the little guy. No one was hurt other than busted lips and a black eye. Don't worry; I'm fine. Not a scratch. Hoping and praying it stays that way. I miss you two terribly. Ruthie, you listen to your mother and help her and your Aunt Jane all you're able. I'll send you a feather, should I find one, to add to your collection. Helen, don't overwork.
Take care of yourself. Give Ed and Jane my regards.
Love you both,
Walter (Father)

Mother's tears fell on the letter and smudged Father's signature. She laid it flat on her vanity so it could dry, and took me into her arms.

"He is a noble man; and he will fight bravely and honorably, and return home to us."

I wanted to assure her as much as she was assuring me, but I had no words. I had only hope, and no voice to give it; only tears.

***

Mother had deliveries to make in town, so I walked with her to help her carry the dresses she had wrapped so neatly in brown paper and tied with string. There were four dresses; all being delivered to the same address. Two sisters, one a widow and the other having never married, had hired Mother to sew dresses for them for their upcoming trip to visit family in Boston. It would be colder there, so they had my mother use heavy fabrics like velvet, and requested long sleeves and high collars. If anyone could accommodate those requests and make a beautiful dress, it was my mother. Her creativity amazed me.

Walking through town, there were always sideways glances and whispers. I was now known as the lion tamer's daughter, thanks to the whip incident. Some people found it admirable that I defended my cousin. Most others thought it deplorable that a young girl would act out in violence. Those people also held my mother accountable for my poor parenting; not once holding themselves or their neighbors accountable for their boys' aggression towards a girl both younger and smaller than them. I was afraid my mother would be ashamed of me, but she just held her head high and walked on.

"Don't give them a second thought," she said, as though she had read my mind. "You did the right thing. You stood up for someone who couldn't defend themselves. Walk proudly, Ruth."

We arrived at the home of the sisters, Ms. Martin and Mrs. Case, also known as Widow Case. Their maid opened the door and escorted us to a sitting room where the sisters greeted us. They were both in their early sixties, and wore their grey hair in fancy arrangements high on their heads; a bit Victorian in style.

"Oh, this is lovely. Simply lovely," said Ms. Martin as she opened one of her dresses.

"Exquisite is the word," added Mrs. Case.

"Thank you. I'm glad you're pleased," Mother said in a modest tone. She was very humble about her talents and found it difficult to accept a compliment.

Ms. Case looked at me, and then cleared her throat. Her sister looked her way, and then looked at me. I could tell there was an unspoken conversation going on between them...and it involved me!

"Pardon our lack of tact, but...are you by chance the lion tamer's daughter?" asked Mrs. Case. Mother seemed to choke on air, and had a coughing fit.

"I am," I stated proudly. Mother quit coughing, but stared at me in horror.

"Let me congratulate you," said Mrs. Case, taking my hand in hers. "You taught those bullies a lesson they won't soon forget. But, let me share with you some advice. Sometimes taking a stand for what is right and good requires a price. Doing the right thing can add a burden to your life. Such as the gossip and foolishness in town concerning you and that whip. But, even so, taking a stand as you did is certainly worth any price you might have to pay. Regret for doing nothing is most costly, and the weight unbearable."

I nodded, but true clarity of her words didn't come to me then. It took a few years for me to fully understand—and value—the wisdom she had shared.

***

Valentine's Day was the following day, and Lizzie was acting a fool over some boy in her class who she hoped would give her a Valentine. She had spent days cutting, gluing and crafting a big red heart with his name on it. I usually just rolled my eyes and let her be.

"You got a letter," Aunt Jane told me, very nonchalant.

"From Father?"

"No, I don't believe so. It's postmarked from Sarasota."

Pulling open the envelope, I found a red paper heart with a purple feather glued to the front. On the back was a handwritten poem:

Roses are red.
Violets are blue.
Sugar is sweet,
And so are you.
Happy Valentine's Day
Albert

"What is that? Who's it from?" squealed Lizzie.
I handed her the card. "It's from Albert."
Lizzie read the poem and smiled, and then gave me a curious look. "Who's Albert?"
I spent the rest of the evening sitting on the screened porch telling Lizzie all about Albert and Pricha, the night his father left for good, and the day we held hands…and the feathers…I showed her my feathers.
"How romantic," she sighed. We both giggled.
Finally sitting in silence, we stared at the stars and dreamt of living happily ever after. For all we knew, there really was such a thing.

CHAPTER TEN

"Alright, you've been stifling your laughter long enough...let it out!" Ruth insisted.

I did as I was told, and wiped the tears from my eyes.

"I can't help it! The image of you going after those bullies with that whip--priceless!"

Ruth covered her mouth as she laughed a little. "You should've seen their faces."

"Oh, how I wish I could!" I said as I jotted down some notes.

"What're you writing?" she asked.

"Just some notes. I'm thinking of compiling a list of life lessons from your story. For instance, today's portion would be 'Stand up for what is right.' Or maybe 'Defend those who can't defend themselves.'"

"A list? No, no, no. That won't do. That's...what do you young people call it? Cheesy! Yes, cheesy."

"Hey, easy with the criticism! I'm a sensitive writer," I teased. "What's wrong with a list of valuable wisdom for life?"

"You shouldn't lay it all out there like that. Tell people a good story, and they'll glean their own lessons. They'll figure out what they're supposed to learn without you spelling it out one by one. In fact, they're more apt to learn the lesson if it's veiled within a story. Jesus was a great teacher, and He taught by parables. There's a reason for that."

I shook my head with understanding. "Got it. More wisdom! And, no list. So, you mentioned Jesus. Does that mean you're a believer?"

"Yes."

"I didn't see you wearing a cross necklace or anything, and you didn't pray over our tea and cookies."

"You're a real smart-ass, you know that?"

Laughter burst out of me like a fog horn. "I'm sorry—I just never expected that. But, that's what I love about you. You're completely unpredictable."

"And that word is in the Bible, by the way," she retorted.

"In reference to a donkey," I shot back. Ruth simply raised one eyebrow at me, and I laughed some more.

***

I was late getting home that night because of a pre-opening interview with a local artist, and the fact that I stopped by Nature's Food Patch Café for some blackened salmon and balsamic red coleslaw to bring home. Over the past six months, I had developed a habit of grabbing fast food which left me feeling crappy. Tonight began a new trend of eating better and feeling better.

Barely had my food on a plate when someone banged on my front door. I knew that bang anywhere.

"Katz, go home!" I yelled.

"I wanna hear the old woman's story!"

"I want to eat a nice meal and go to bed!"

"I brought wine!"

I opened the door. "This isn't because of the wine. It's because I don't want my neighbors calling the police 'cause of all your yelling."

"My yelling? You yelled, too! And, you know you want some wine to go with your..."

"Salmon."

"Ooooh. Somebody's eating fancy."

"Just got sick of pizza and chow mein."

"You go ahead and start eating. I'll pour the wine."

Katz pulled two glasses from a reusable grocery bag, and a bottle of Chardonnay; and sat on my thrift store sofa. I took my recorder out from my backpack, and hit the play button. We sat and listened through every recording of Ruth's story without saying a word.

"Wow. Great story. Really. This could turn into something publishable. Not in our artsy little publication, but you know…a book or something," Katz commented.

"Possibly."

"There's sharing some great wisdom—the kind only people her age can share."

"True, but no list."

Katz looked at me with a confused look. "No what?"

"Never mind."

Katz drank his last sip of wine. "Well, I'd better get going. I don't suppose you have any news on our case?"

"None. But, maybe no news is good news."

Katz cackled. "Ha! We couldn't be so lucky."

***

The ringing of my cell phone woke me up at seven; which really aggravated me since my alarm was set for seven-fifteen.

"Hello?" I'm sure I slurred a little as I spoke.

"Is this Michael Tallen?"

"Yeah." I said as I wiped some slobber from my cheek.

"This is District Attorney Carolyn Nelson's office. She needs to speak with you. Are you available this morning?"

"*This* morning?" I asked, hoping my inflection would buy me a little more time. It didn't.

"She has nine-o'clock open."

I sighed. "Yeah, alright. I'll be there at nine."

***

Bonnie instinctively knew my hot shower had not sufficiently woke me, and took me straight to 9th Bar for a double espresso and a muffin. I'm pretty sure that Banana nut counts as health food.

Once I arrived at the D.A.'s office, the butterflies in my stomach unfurled their wings and began to flutter incessantly. For a brief moment, I thought I might lose that banana nut muffin in their potted fake palm tree.

"I'm Michael Tallen," I told the receptionist.

"Yes, Sir. She's expecting you," she replied, nodding towards an office door to her right.

I stepped inside and took a seat. She shuffled some papers on her desk, and took a sip of coffee.

"Mr. Tallen, thank you for coming on such short notice. I'm sure you're wondering why I asked you here."

"I have my suspicions."

"We are re-opening the case which you helped to bring to fruition."

"May I ask why?"

"You may ask, but I can't give you an answer...not yet. It's an ongoing investigation."

"How exactly am I involved?" My voice cracked. I was getting more nervous.

"I need you, first of all, to verify some information you initially shared with us. Then, I may need to ask you a few more questions." She shuffled some more papers. "Ready?"

"No. I mean, am I under investigation or am I just helping you with an investigation?" I tried to remember if I had stored my lawyer's number in my cell phone.

"Just as you were a witness in the case originally, you are a witness now. Why? Should we be investigating you?"

"No, no. It's just that…I thought maybe there was some retaliation going on."

She smiled and relaxed, leaning back in her chair. "Mr. Tallen, I for one consider your actions heroic. If there is one thing I would never permit to happen on my watch, it would be retaliation for exposing police corruption. You are simply a witness, and we need every bit of information you've got. Is that clear enough for you?"

The tenseness in my neck and shoulders let up. "Yes. Thank you. Now, what do you need to know?"

***

After my meeting with District Attorney Nelson, I stood outside, leaning against Bonnie, and called Ben.

"Maupin," he answered.

"Ben, it's Mike. Gotta sec?"

"Just a sec. I'm assuming you've got news about our case."

"A little. I met with the D.A. this morning, and she told me they have officially reopened the case and that there's an ongoing investigation. She also assured me that I was just a witness. I had to verify some information I had already given them, and answer a few new questions."

"New questions about what?"

"I had to promise not to share that information with anyone."

"Are you kidding me?"

"Sorry, man. But, I can tell you that there's no retaliation involved. They just have some additional suspects."

"That still doesn't settle my nerves any."

"I know. I mean, I don't want to have to testify and go through all that again. But, if I have to…"

"I hope to God she doesn't call me into her office. That could cause me way more problems than just you going in."

"I thought about that. Maybe that's why she hasn't asked you for a meeting."

"Yet."

"Try not to sweat it. I know it could be another big hassle, but it's the right thing to do," I said, attempting to encourage him.

"Yeah, yeah. Remind me of that when I'm up in the middle of the night with a migraine and an ulcer."

***

It was time for another meeting with Ruth, and I was happy to have the distraction. My mind kept wandering off—imagining as many "what if" moments regarding the case as it could muster up.

Our meeting was set for eight-thirty with plans to share breakfast, but I arrived ten minutes early and had already had an espresso.

While waiting in the bedroom still cluttered with boxes of keepsakes, I thumbed through some stacks of photographs and postcards. As I set one stack back inside a box, I noticed a copied newspaper article on the bed. It was from the archives, and it was about my case!

"Sorry to keep you waiting," Ruth apologized as she walked into the room.

I was torn between asking her about the article or just ignoring it…or maybe even snooping around some more when we took a break.

"No worries. I'm early."

"They'll have breakfast ready in a short while. Biscuits and tomato gravy."

I chuckled. "You knew I couldn't resist trying that after hearing your story about cooking with Aunt Jane. That had my stomach growling and my mouth watering."

"This looks like a particularly good batch of gravy. You should enjoy it. In the meantime, I have an idea of where we should pick-up with this story of mine."

I sat down and prepared my recorder. That article could wait 'til later. "Alright, little miss whip-wonder, what on earth could you possibly do next?"
She found that amusing. "You'll just have to listen. I have to keep you guessing." Ruth sat down and closed her eyes, and I pressed the record button.

"Whenever you're ready," I prompted.

"Well...it was the summer of 1943, and we had gone to a little carnival with games and sideshows..."

"Breakfast's ready!" came a yell from the living room.

I stopped the recorder and escorted Ruth to the kitchen table. My plate hosted two biscuits topped with a ladle-full of tomato gravy; and when I had finished eating, there was barely a hint any food had been placed on that plate at all.

"That was delicious—amazing, really. I've never had anything like it."

Ruth smiled, and I could tell she was pleased. Mr. and Mrs. Wilson, the late Lizzie's daughter and son-in-law, were equally pleased.

"The recipe has been passed down, and thankfully, so has the skill," Ruth complimented her second cousin.

We made our way back to the room, and settled once again into our seats.

"Now, where was I?" she asked me.

"Summer of 1943...at the carnival," I reminded her.

Ruth nodded and chortled, "Oh, yes. I remember it like yesterday."

CHAPTER ELEVEN

Lizzie and I wore dresses my mother had made us from flour sacks. Mine was a blue floral, and Lizzie's was green and yellow; which went beautifully with her red hair. I admit I was a tad jealous of Lizzie because she was so pretty, and her hair caught everyone's attention. My looks were more common—ordinary, and that was exactly how I felt.

The two of us were walking along, sharing a pink cotton candy, and stopping to play some of the silly games like ring toss or target shooting. I loved this carnival because it reminded me of the midway of the circus; especially the side shows with their barkers inviting you to "step right up!" The atmosphere was busy and noisy, the crowd a bit boisterous, and the sights and sounds almost overwhelming. It felt like home.

"Step right up, gentleman, and test your strength! Demonstrate your muscle for your gal—show us what ya got!" cried one barker.

"I wanna give it a try!" Lizzie yelled.

The barker laughed. The object of the game was to swing an oversized hammer and hit the lever so that the puck is forced up the tall tower and rings the bell at the top. We had seen two men attempt the game, and neither one had made it more than three quarters of the way.

"Lizzie, this game is for men," I scolded her.

"Says who?" Lizzie grabbed the hammer from the barker's hand, and got herself into position.

"Hold on," I called out. "You'll never get it to the top on your own. Let me help!"

"Wait a minute, now,' the barker said, holding up his hand to stop us. "This game is for one person."

"Says who?" asked Lizzie. I had to giggle.

"Let them have a try!" called out a spectator. The barker let us take hold of the hammer, and together we swung with all might and rung the bell. A small crowd of people had gathered to watch us, and they all cheered and clapped their hands. Even the barker smiled and applauded, and gave us a prize…a stuffed monkey, dressed as a bellhop in a red and white striped uniform complete with hat. We named him Mickey the Monkey, and took turns carrying him around the carnival.

Off to the side of the main path, a bunch of people had swarmed around a young man. He looked to be about sixteen, had long black hair; and was dressed in a tribal costume with feathers and bright-colored beads. He let out a yelp that sounded like a wild animal, garnering the attention of everyone within a hundred-yard radius.

"I am Hothlepoya, a Creek Seminole! My name means "crazy warrior," and I was given this name because of my absurd level of bravery which I will now demonstrate to you."

This boy then sat on the back of a live alligator, grabbed its mouth—holding it shut, and wrestled this gator until he had it sufficiently tied up with rope. The audience applauded, and some threw coins into a pair of moccasins that sat on the ground nearby.

"That was…interesting," commented Lizzie.

"More like appalling," I criticized. Lizzie gave me a curious look.

We walked closer to the boy and the gator as the rest of the people dispersed.

"You can come closer," said the Seminole boy. "I will keep you safe from the gator."

He must have noticed my bored facial expression because he then asked, "Aren't you impressed?"

"Not really," I replied.

"But, I wrestled this gator! I tied him up—just to keep you safe."

"First of all, you didn't tie him up to keep anyone safe. You tied him up to earn money. Second of all, you shouldn't treat your animal that way. And finally, that was the most atrocious attempt at a sideshow attraction I've ever seen."

He just stared at me in shock.

"You should let me help you," I told him.

"Why would I let you help me? I don't need help with this gator."

"Not with the gator," I replied. "With your show. I know all about putting on a good show and keeping the crowd entertained. You should let me help you."

Now, he was angry. "I told you I don't need your help! If you don't like my gator show, then go away!"

Lizzie pulled my arm, and started leading me back onto the main path.

"Suit yourself!" I yelled as I walked away.

***

"What was wrong with his show?" Lizzie asked.

"Too short. No build-up! He should take his time and convince people the gator is dangerous—build anticipation for what he will do next. His costume was horrible; certainly not authentic, and that tells the audience you're a fake."

"But he was a fake, right?"

"Not completely. He's obviously an Indian, and he definitely knows how to handle a gator. He just doesn't know how to make it entertaining."

"I bet you learned all this stuff from your father."

"I did," I said with a hint of sadness. "I sure do miss him."

"Maybe you'll get another letter soon," Lizzie encouraged me, and handed me Mickey the Monkey.

***

After a long walk home that evening, I was elated to find that I had not one, but two letters—one from my father, and one from Albert. This day couldn't have gotten any better.

Father told us his management skills were being put to good use with rationing food and supplies for his fellow soldiers. He didn't tell us any of the awful happenings that we knew about through the newspaper and radio. Father always wrote about good things except for a vague line or two about how terrible war was, in general.

This time, he had included an auburn-colored feather; believed to be from some kind of hawk. I immediately placed it in my tobacco tin with the rest of my collection.

Albert had been writing once a week, and I always wrote back; scenting my stationary with some of mother's perfume. We wrote to each other about every day happenings. He told me about Pricha's new tricks, new foods he tried in new cities while traveling with his new circus. I told him about chasing bullies with whips and walks into town with Lizzie to buy candy. Now, I had something really interesting to write about…an Indian boy who wrestles gators.

In my letter to Albert, I told him how lack-luster this boy's performance was—no showmanship, just sit on the gator, grab its mouth closed, and expect applause. His costume looked cheap and didn't fit him right. My list of complaints went on for a while before I realized how badly I wanted to help this young performer.

My father had taught me a lot about managing acts; not specific lessons, but by observation, I had picked up on what made an act entertaining. Albert was definitely an entertainer. He and Pricha had ways of hooking the crowd into a "what might happen next" frenzy. This so-called Crazy Warrior kid, on the other hand, needed help…my help.

***

The next day was a Sunday, and I went to church with my mother, aunt, uncle, and Lizzie; even though I still wasn't so sure about becoming a regular attendee. On the road, we had Sunday afternoon performances to prepare for; so my father would sometimes just read some Scripture and say a prayer before starting work. And, even that wasn't all the time.

Still, the little First Baptist Church on the corner wasn't so bad, and at least I was a good ways closer to the fair when service let out. The final amen was barely spoken when Lizzie and I made a dash for the door, headed straight for the games and exhibitions. Lizzie wanted to play the strength game again, and ring the bell for another stuffed monkey. I promised we'd do that after I spoke with the Indian boy.

"Hothlepooya," she said.

"No, that's not it. Holapaya," I attempted.

"Not even close. We'll just have to ask him."

"I'm sure he'll say it again when he says his pitiful little introduction."

"Why are you so critical?" Lizzie asked.

I stopped walking and faced her. "It's just pitiful. He's getting pocket change from folks, and not a lot of it either. If I can get him to change a few things, and make his show more appealing; he'll earn a lot more money."

"I see. You really are trying to help."

"Yes! And, besides, it irks me to see a bad performance when I know how simple it is to make it a good one."

"Simple for you, maybe. You know all about this stuff," Lizzie reminded me.

"That's why I need to talk to this boy—share what I know—like a teacher."

Lizzie nodded, and we kept walking.

Sure enough, there he was giving his five-second speech, and going after that gator who looked as bored as I was. The handful of people standing around barely clapped and walked off; tossing a few coins his direction.

"Hey, you!" I called out.

"I have a name. Hothlepoya."

"Yeah, I heard—Crazy Warrior. Listen, I'd be willing to help you with your act so you can earn more money."

"Help me? How on earth could you help me?"

"Her daddy runs a whole big circus," Lizzie bragged; albeit a bit untruthfully.

"So? That doesn't mean you can help me."

"Yes, it does," I began to explain. "My father taught me everything he knows about how to put on a good show. And your show ain't good."

He scowled at me, and walked off.

"I think you made him mad," Lizzie observed.

I shrugged. "Guess I can't force him to take my help."

We started to walk towards the games when we heard footsteps coming up fast behind us.

"Alright, alright," said the Indian boy. "I barely made any money today; so if you really think you can help me...then, tell me what I need to do."

"First of all, tell me your real name because I can't pronounce that other one," I demanded.

"James. James Cypress. My father is an elder for the Seminole Tribe, and Hothlepoya really is my name, too."

"Fine, but I'm gonna call you James. We'll come back here after we go win a stuffed monkey," I told him.

He gave us a curious look, and watched us walk off.

***

When we arrived back at James' exhibition, there were no spectators. James sat there by the gator looking forlorn.

"Cotton candy?" Lizzie offered him. He took a pinch, and nodded his appreciation.

"I see you won your monkey," he said, waving towards our cute, little bell hop.

"Yes, but we aren't allowed back," I admitted. James chuckled.

"You gonna tell me how to fix my show or what?" he asked.

"I'm not just gonna tell you. I'm gonna show you!"

For the next half hour, I taught James how to barker for himself; how to stand and motion with his hands; how to demonstrate respect and fear of his gator so that his actions were more awe-inspiring; and how to build anticipation.

"You're too quick!" I complained. "And you act like it's no big deal. If it's no big deal, then why do they care to see it? And why would they give you money to see it? You've got to talk about how dangerous the gator is—how he's a man-eater and such."

"Alright...I get it. Make it exciting."

"Exactly! And one more thing," I said pulling on his sleeve. "Take off your shirt."

Lizzie gasped and James' eyes grew wide.

"I'm gonna take it to my mother. She's a seamstress, and she can fix it."

"It doesn't need fixed! There's no holes or nothin'."

"It's not right. Just…trust me."

James took off his shirt, and handed it to me.

"I'm supposed to start performing at noon tomorrow," he informed me.

"I'll have it back by then," I said, and Lizzie and I headed for home.

***

It was dusk when Lizzie and I got home, and Mother wasn't too happy with me for not being home to help with supper.

"Last night was fine, but two nights in a row of missin' chores is a problem," she scolded me.

"Yes, ma'am."

"And what is this you're carrying?" she asked, pointing to James' shirt.

"Um…it's a shirt."

"I can see that. Looks like some sort of costume."

"Yes, ma'am," I opened it up and showed it to her.   "It belongs to this boy at the fair. He's a Seminole Indian. But, Momma, his costume is…"

"Pitiful," she said, taking the shirt from my hands.

"He needs your help," I pleaded. "I helped him with this act, but only you can save this shirt."

Momma laughed heartily. "You helped him with his act?"

"Oh, yes, ma'am," began Lizzie. "You should'a seen her—do this, say that, stand this-a-way. She was amazing."

I was a little embarrassed. "He wasn't earning any money because he wasn't entertaining," I explained.

My mother smiled at me with something I had only seen once—when I took the whip to those bullies…pride. She was proud of me for helping James.

"I'll see what I can do," she said, and carried the shirt off to her room.

"You won't believe it when you see it," I told Lizzie. "She'll have him looking better than any Alligator wrestling Indian out there."

***

The next morning, I stepped into the kitchen to make coffee before the sun was even up. There, resting on the back of a kitchen chair, was newly sewn shirt. Mother hadn't simply fixed-up the shirt I brought to her. No, she had made an entirely new shirt. This one was pieced together from animal hide and naturally-dyed fabric with hand-woven trim. From the sight of the kitchen, my mother had used tea and berries to stain the fabrics; giving them a more authentic look. This shirt was amazing.

I cleaned up the little bit of remaining mess in the kitchen, made coffee, and wrapped the shirt in brown paper like we did the dresses she made. What a gift I had for James!

When I arrived at the fair, James was standing with a group of Seminole men. The only reason I knew they were Indian was because of their hair. They wore slacks and dress shirts just like my father. No feathers or moccasins or anything that resembled the image I associated with Seminole Indian men.

They spoke in hushed tones so that I couldn't hear them as I approached. Once they saw that I was waiting to speak with James, they nodded to me and walked away without saying a word. I was too enthralled to say anything, and quickly realized I had been standing there with my mouth open like an idiot.

"Who was that?" I asked James, still awe-struck.

"Some of the Elder Council of our tribe. The tallest one there," he pointed, "is my father."

"He looks important."

"He is…at least to us. Wouldn't matter much to you, I don't guess."

I didn't understand what he meant by that.

"I brought you something special," I told him, handing him the package.

James tore open the paper, and unfolded the shirt; eyeing it carefully.

"Is something wrong?" I asked, curious about his silence.

"No, not at all. This is...really something. It looks like a shirt my father has for special ceremonies. Where'd you get this?"

"I didn't get it anywhere! My mother made it. She was up half the night dying fabric and weaving that trim."

"Amazing."

"That's the word I use all the time...about my momma's sewing."

He put on the shirt, and it fit him like a glove. I don't know how mother even knew—maybe she just got lucky.

"Now, let's do a run-through," I instructed. "Show me what you've got."

James cleared his throat, and stood on a bottle crate covered with twigs and leaves.

"Step up, ladies and gentlemen, to witness a death-defying feat! I, Hothlepoya—meaning Crazy Warrior—will war against a man-eating alligator to protect you, the innocent bystander!"

"Not bad, so far," I commented.

We spent another twenty minutes tweaking his speech and his exaggerated movements while wrestling the gator. It wasn't perfect, but it was certainly an improvement.

I shook his hand, and began my walk back home. My job there was done. But, that made me sad. I wanted to do more. I wanted to help more. I wanted to stay around James the crazy warrior.

***

That evening, we were sitting on the front porch listening to the radio when two shadowy figures approached the house. One was tall, the other was about my height. As they entered the dim glow of the yellow porch light, I recognized James and his father.

"Hello, there," Uncle Ed spoke to the strangers.

"Hello," replied Mr. Cypress. "Pardon us for interrupting your evening. We were told this is the residence of the seamstress who made this," he said, pointing to James' shirt he was wearing.

"Yes, Sir. That's my work," replied my mother.

"Thank you, ma'am," said James. "You have my sincere appreciation."

"It is a work of art. Excellent craftsmanship," complimented Mr. Cypress.

"Thank you so much. Ruth here wanted you to have something to, um…enhance your performance."

Mr. Cypress grunted—a sound that seemed like disapproval to me, but I couldn't be sure.

"You are very kind. Allow me to pay you for your hard work," he offered.

"No, Sir. It is my gift. I used to be able to create more unique pieces like this until I had to start sewing for the upper class to provide for my family. It was a labor of love, and I couldn't take a penny for it."

Mr. Cypress nodded in silence, grabbed James' shoulder, and they walked off.

"I don't think he's too happy with that boy of his," Uncle Ed observed.

"Maybe he doesn't want him performing," mother said, looking at me.
"Maybe not. But, I bet he made twice as much money today, wearing that shirt," I said, matter-of-factly.

***

With the full moon shining in through our gauzy curtains, and the distant sound of Uncle Ed snoring; I sat up in bed next to mother and embraced the sadness that had been trying to overcome me for days. I missed my father. I missed Albert…and Pricha. I missed my circus family. I missed traveling. And now, I was going to miss James and maybe even his gator wrestling.

Tears ran down my cheeks, and I resorted to using the sleeve of my nightgown to wipe my runny nose. Mother shifted positions in her sleep; so I got out of bed and sat in the cane-back chair positioned by the window so as not to disturb her further. Leaning my head against the wall, I could peer through the small space between the curtain and the wall and see out the window. The other houses with their little gardens like ours, sheds for tools, and a clothesline across the yard were lined up in a row. Only a handful of windows revealed a glow of light. Most people in this neighborhood were asleep.

Most people had to go to work or keep their house and care for children the next day. Most people were accustomed to this life of staying in one place, and living where the unexpected rarely occurred. I was discovering that I was not most people.

I wanted my father back home. And, I wanted our circus back together with all our performing families, crewmen and animals. I wanted Lizzie to go with us (but of course her parents would never allow that). I wanted Albert to hold my hand and give me feathers…and kisses. I wanted James…I wanted a lot of things.

After almost an hour of my self-pity party, I crawled back into bed, and put my hope in something I heard at Uncle Ed and Aunt Jane's

Baptist church, "Weeping may endure for a night, but joy cometh in the morning."

CHAPTER TWELVE

"**I must say**, Ruth, I'm getting the feeling there's a love triangle in the making with you, Albert and James." I told her, teasing just a bit.

"Nonsense," she replied. Her face was turning two shades of red.

"You can dismiss it if you want, but I know there's some great romance in this story of yours. I'll change the subject, though. Your father had obviously influenced you a great deal. You really stepped up and took charge, and taught this Native American kid how to perform. That's really something!"

"Some would say I was too forward...bossy even."

I shrugged. "Maybe. But, you don't seem to be one to put much stock in what other people think of you."

"Not really," Ruth admitted.

"And think of the valuable lesson you taught Lizzie, as well, when you helped her with the strength test game."

"Oh, you're not going to add to that list of yours, are you?"

I laughed. "No, no, I tossed the list in the trash. You were right. It was cheesy."

"Lizzie taught me valuable lessons, too. We were good for each other. I like to think so, anyway. But, there's no more time for stories. I have some appointments today, and I'm sure you have writing to do."

"Speaking of which," I hesitated, second-guessing myself about proceeding with this question. "I noticed you have an article that I had written…from the archives."

"Oh, yes. I have a few," she confessed. "I did a little research before choosing you to write my story."

"O.k. But-"

"No more, now. I've got to get ready for my appointments. I'll see you Thursday. Off you go!"

Ruth had never ushered me out so fast. She was hiding something from me, and it bothered me to no end. But, what bothered me even more was the notification on my phone of a missed call from the district attorney's office.

I could feel a migraine coming on. I hopped on Bonnie and weighed the pros and cons of going out of my way to get another espresso. Who was I kidding? I went for coffee.

***

"You know," said the barista standing in front of the giant octopus mural, "we have other coffees, and teas, too. If you're in the mood to be adventurous... you could try something new."

"I'm more of a stick-to-what-I-like kind of guy. And, I'm definitely not in an adventurous mood."

"Ah. You're in need of a comfort fix. I get it. The usual then."

"Some things never change," said a voice from behind me. "This guy drinks so much of your double espresso, it should be named after him."

"Ben? What're you doing here?" I asked, a little shocked.

"I'll tell you over coffee. Make that two usuals, please." He said holding up two fingers like he was making a peace sign.

We got our drinks and sat on wooden barstools near the wall with the octopus.

"It gives me the creeps," I told Ben, nodding toward the painting of the eight legged sea creature.

"What? Why? I think she's cute."

"Tentacles are not cute."

"Whatever."

"So, are you going to tell me what you're doing here?" I asked as I blew on my steaming concoction.

"I was actually going to come by your office, and remembered you telling me how often you came here. Figured I could use caffeine anyway; so I came in and…surprise!"

"Probably a good thing you're here to talk. I have to return a call to the D.A.'s office."

"I was there yesterday. They had me go over all my previous testimony. Didn't you do that already?"

"Yeah. I don't know what's up now. I hate this. I mean, I know they're going after some bigger fish now. Remember how bad it was when we were just trying to prove cops were corrupt? What's it going to be like if we're involved in proving some elected official is corrupt?"

"Hell. It's going to be like hell," Ben replied dryly.
We both took sips of our espresso, and sat in silence for a few moments.

"But," Ben began, "think of what those boys who were falsely accused went through. Behind bars. Brutal fights. And, they were innocent."

I hung my head, feeling ashamed of my self-pity. "Yeah. We're doing the right thing."

"I'll drink to that," Ben joked, and finished off his coffee.

***

Having returned the call, another meeting was scheduled for four in the afternoon. My second encounter with D.A. Carolyn Nelson, and I was just as anxious as the first time. Maybe it was some form of PTSD, having surviving all those visits to the principal's office as a kid. I sat in the same chair, and bounced one leg nervously.

"Mr. Tallen, you can relax. You're not in trouble."

"Sorry," I apologized as I purposed myself to calm down and sit still, "So what are we talking about today?"

"This morning my office filed charges of corruption, including bribery and extortion, against the deputy mayor."

"Aw, man," I sighed heavily and bent over, resting my elbows on my knees.

"We have evidence against some of the mayor's staff, as well. And, charges have been brought against former police chief, Reed."

"This is huge." I could feel beads of sweat forming on my forehead.

"Yes, it is. Your testimony and evidence helped because it corroborated information we gathered from other witnesses and through search warrants."

"That's great. Really. So, why am I here?"

"I was hoping you might be able to help me with something."

"Uh-oh." Now, I was feeling really uneasy.

"The boys who were falsely accused—you and Detective Maupin."

"Lieutenant," I corrected.

"Right. He's now a Lieutenant. As I was saying, the two of you once managed those boys' friends and families to come forward and testify. Do you think you could do it again?"

I shook my head and kind of snickered. "That was mostly Ben's work. He had a connection with those people from working so close to the reservation, and he had rapport with the reservation police. I was just his assistant, basically."

"Fine. But, do you think you two could do it again? We need more of them to come forward with information to solidify our case."

Another heavy sigh escaped my mouth. "You mean to tell me that there are people on the Seminole reservation who can testify against our deputy mayor?"

"Yes. And Reed, who was the chief of police at the time, and at least two members of the mayor's staff."

I ran my hand through my hair, and leaned back in the chair. That migraine was trying to come back. "I just don't know that we can pull this off. Can't speak for Ben, really, but for myself...I haven't been on the reservation in a long time. The Seminole people-" I stopped speaking, and there was absolute silence. A thought had occurred to me.

"What about the Seminole people?" she asked, forcing me back into my original train of thought.

"They're not easily persuaded to get involved outside of their tribe. They consider this our problem—not theirs."

"This is as much their problem as anyone's. Their boys were being singled out, and their people have suffered because of this corruption. We can prove it." She said before leaning back into her high backed, leather chair.

"I'll talk to Ben," I acquiesced, hoping to at least buy myself some time. "Maybe he still has some connections. Maybe we can help you. Maybe—no promises."

"I'll accept that."

I left her office, and went straight home. No supper. Didn't even get out of my clothes. I just landed face first on my bed and went to sleep.

***

I woke up at two in the morning with a dry mouth and aching back; and made a mental note to never sleep on my stomach with my feet hanging off the bed again.

Stumbling into the kitchen for a bottle of water, I remembered the thought I had about the Seminole tribe. Ruth had the archived articles about the original case, and the story she had shared...could there possibly be a connection? I shook it off as delirium from stress and an awkward sleeping position. Coincidence, I decided. This is Florida, and there's a lot that involves Seminoles. Besides, Ruth had admitted she researched me as a writer. I still didn't understand why, but in the wee hours of the morning, it didn't really matter. I drank my water and went back to bed, hoping for more sleep this time.

***

Waking up, again, at six-thirty to the annoying alarm on my phone; I opted for a quick shower to perk me up. Then—before even having coffee—I called Ben.

"I take it you've got some info for me," Ben answered, knowing it was me calling.

"The D.A. wants you and me to entice witnesses to help her case."

I shouldn't repeat the words Ben used to convey his feelings about this. Let's just say he was less than enthusiastic. Much less.

"That's what I was thinking," I admitted.

"Don't get me wrong, I understand her asking us to 'rally the troops' to go after these guys; but I don't think she understands what we endured the first time."

"Probably not, but…" I hesitated.

"But, what?" Ben pressed.

"Yeah, we went through heck. We were slandered, mocked, bullied…but, it all worked out in the end. We were vindicated, and the victims got justice. So, I guess I'm wondering why we're so worked-up about doing it again."

"Because all that slander, mockery and bullying took its toll. It was a war, and for several months, we were on the losing side."

"Yeah, but when did we become such wusses?" Ben laughed. "You did not just call me a wuss."

"Yes, I did. But, to be fair, I called myself one, as well."

He sighed, and I remained silent to let him think. "You're right. I mean, journalists go to war-torn third world countries all the time. The least you can do is encourage some victims to speak out against their oppressors. Geez, man." He finally said.

This time I laughed. "Yeah, well, you're a cop. Your job description includes dealing with dangerous bad guys and helping people in need. So, you gonna do your job or not?"

We agreed to meet on Saturday and canvas the neighborhoods where we knew people, and thought we could make some headway.

***

Being a Lieutenant, Ben had to be careful how he approached the Seminole people, even off the reservation. If he flashed his badge or used too much pressure, they could not only shy away from talking to us; but they could accuse him of over-stepping and notify the reservation police. That would be a sticky situation. Besides, we weren't trying to get testimonies ourselves. We were simply there to encourage them to come forward and talk with the district attorney if they had valuable information.

One person we both we knew well was Marie Weatherford. Her ancestors, like many Seminole, were Scottish and Creek; and one ancestor, William, led the Creek War against the United States.

Marie was a respected woman of her tribe and her community; college-educated thanks to her own tenacity. She mentored youth and advocated for the needs of her people. Sadly, Marie's oldest grandson had been arrested while participating in a brutal street fight. Additional charges were filed, however, thanks to drugs planted on him by a corrupt and racist cop; looking to get "Indian hoodlums" off the street, and give the police chief a victory in his supposed war on drugs.

"Marie, it's good to see you. You're looking well," Ben greeted her.

"I wish I could say it is good to see the two of you, but, honestly, you're being here is making me nervous."

"I'm so sorry," I sincerely apologized. "We know the last thing you want to do is re-live all that happened with your grandson."

"But…" She knew we had a purpose for seeking her out.

"But, we've been asked to help encourage anyone who might have more to share about things they've witnessed to please come forward. The District Attorney's office has built a strong case against some elected officials, but she needs more of you to tell your stories…"

"To be snitches," Marie clarified.

"Yes—although I don't like that term. It has a negative connotation."

"And it could have negative consequences. What if we share our 'stories' as you put it, and these officials seek revenge?" She asked with more than a little fear in her voice.

"We'll protect you," Ben promised her. "I have friends on the reservation, and we can work together to protect anyone who speaks up."

"I can see about writing some articles for the paper. If anyone is comfortable having their name and image published, it might reassure them. Being out in the open, and very public, can actually shield you."

"Because if one of us turned up dead it would be suspicious," Marie spoke bluntly.

"Let's not go there. No one ever got death threats before," Ben tried to calm her.

"We weren't going after the higher-ups before."

I stood there speechless because I couldn't offer any other assurances. We had said all we could say, and apparently we weren't convincing.

After three hours of this kind of conversation with various people, we decided to end our campaign and head home.

"I don't know why we were even asked to do this," said Ben. "We have no official capacity in this case, and have nothing to offer them. Even my oath of protection is a bit bogus. I mean, I don't even work in this district anymore."

"I know. But, the sentiment was true. You would do whatever you could to protect them. All I could offer them was publicity in hopes it would scare away any would-be assassin."

Ben got a laugh out of that. "I seriously doubt the deputy mayor would try to have someone killed."

"I don't know, man. This is a crazy world these days."

"Don't I know it? Don't I know it?"

Ben left, and I hopped on Bonnie to go by the market café and pick up more of that salmon. If only Katz would stop by with some wine. Of course when I actually want him to come by unannounced he doesn't. Typical.

***

Thursday morning, I arrived to my meeting with Ruth with a large coffee in hand; even though I had downed a double espresso with my banana nut muffin at 9th Bar. I sat in my usual chair, leaned back and yawned. When I put my hand to my face to cover my yawn, I realized I had forgotten to shave.

"You look a mess," Ruth said when she came into the room.

"Good morning to you, too."

"Your hair's all messy and you haven't shaved. Are you hung over?"

"No, ma'am," I chortled. "It's just been a long week."

"I see."

"So, what's next on our journey, Miss Ruth?" I asked before taking another sip of coffee.

"Well, there's more to tell about James…if you're interested."

"James…You mean Hothlepoya, the gator wrestling kid? Of course I'm interested!"

"Alright. First, we should start with what I know about James' father…"

CHAPTER THIRTEEN

James' father, Mr. Cypress, was a tribal council member of the Florida Seminole tribe, and an incredibly skilled carpenter. He believed in using one's talents, but didn't see any value in James' "talent" for gator wrestling.

Mr. Cypress' Seminole name was "Malatche," meaning "war chief." This was because he had successfully arbitrated between two factions of the tribe; resolving a year-long conflict. That was a decade ago, and the reason he was chosen for the tribal council. He valued his heritage, and felt those who catered to tourists and their perceptions of Native Americans, cheapened their history— disgraced their tribe.

***

I went to the fair on its final day in hopes of seeing James perform with all the elements of showmanship I had taught him. To my surprise, he wasn't there. I walked past the grassy area where he sat atop that gator and declared himself the victor, but he hadn't moved further down. I went back towards the main path with all its games and barkers, but he wasn't there either.

The crowd was getting larger; making it more difficult to navigate my way through in a hurry. Finally deciding to do one last check at his normal spot, I began to walk that direction when I heard a familiar voice.

"It is not a disgrace! It is a demonstration of our skill with wild animals."

"It is a performance…"

"What's wrong with a performance? We perform dances and drumming…"

"Stop arguing!" Mr. Cypress' bass voice carried across the crowded path. He noticed people's glances as they passed by, and calmed himself.

"You are coming home with me, and there will not be further discussion," he demanded of James.

"Father, please, I make good money with this. I'm simply demonstrating a survival skill passed down to us by our ancestors. Consider it…educational."

"That is exactly the same pathetic justification your uncle Charles gave for living in that ridiculous village at Silver Springs, building canoes as a sideshow for tourists."

"It's a working village, and it shows people how amazing our way of life was…and is, and…"

"Enough." This time Mr. Cypress' voice was about an octave lower, quiet, and much more intense.

James must have felt the heat of his father's breath because he stopped talking and took a step backwards.

I had been standing nearby, trying to blend into the crowd as people moved around me. But, suddenly, the crowd thinned and I felt exposed. James turned and saw me, and acted embarrassed.

"Excuse me," I interjected as I stepped toward them. "I was wondering if you'd be giving that amazing demonstration with the gator again. My little cousin and I told some of her friends about it, and they were very interested. I figure it's better than them wasting their time on these silly games. At least your performance is…educational."

James gave me a slight grin. I looked up at Mr. Cypress and smiled as warmly as I could. He gave me a strange look, and then looked at James who was now staring at the ground, avoiding his father's gaze.

"Today is the last day," Mr. Cypress announced. "Best get your friends here soon."

"Yes, sir," I said as I ran off to get Lizzie, and hopefully, a handful of her friends.

***

An hour later, I returned with Lizzie, Uncle Ed and Aunt Jane, Mother, four of Lizzie's friends, and six more children that had been outside playing and decided to follow along. We were such a large group, standing there waiting on James and his gator; that other people thought we must surely be waiting for something exciting, and so the audience grew to almost triple our original little gathering.

Mr. Cypress and another important-looking Indian man stood off to the side, observing everything. James—Hothlepoya—put on a great show. He introduced himself with showmanship, built anticipation, convinced the spectators they were in harm's way near this vicious gator, and took his time wrestling the beast before declaring his victory. I was so proud.

Everyone cheered and clapped. Coins and even some bills were tossed into the moccasins to the point of overflowing. I had told my mother, aunt and uncle about Mr. Cypress' disapproval of James; so they each made a point to commend James on his performance, and how "informative" and "educational" his demonstration had been.

"My husband, Ruth's father, worked with animals," my mother told James and Mr. Cypress, who had stepped closer to hear the conversation. "He was a lion-tamer with the circus; and he has always felt that he was providing a service to his audience—not just entertainment, but a demonstration of the majesty and strength of the lions. He treated his animals with respect; not as property. And when others see that, they in turn treat these animals with respect. I believe that is a value that your people share—treating the land and animals with the respect they deserve."

Mother was brilliant. She effectively argued for James' cause. I could see Mr. Cypress' face soften, and he looked at my mother with admiration.

"Your husband no longer works with lions?" he asked.

"No. He is currently fighting in the war."

"When you hear from him, give him our regards. We pray he comes home safely."

"Thank you."

With that, we parted ways. I whispered a quick "good job" to James, and he winked at me. My heart skipped a beat, and my face felt flushed. Then I thought about Albert. What would he think of my reaction?

"Oh, dear," I whispered to myself.

"What was that?" mother asked.

"Nothing," I lied.

***

That night, when it was good and dark and most people were asleep; I heard a commotion in the back yard. Always curious, I slipped on my robe and went out the back door to see what was going on.

"You shouldn't come out in the dark by yourself," whispered a voice from the darkness. "But, I'm glad you did." James said as he stepped onto the porch, still wearing his performance clothes and moccasins.

"What're you doing here?" I asked, motioning him off the porch and out into the yard where we couldn't be so easily seen.

"I came to see you. You helped me so much, and I don't even know why."

"Just because. It was the right thing to do. You're trying to earn money, and you want to show people your talents. I know all about that."

"I guess you do, being the daughter of a lion tamer and all. I thought your father was in charge of the circus."

"He had to quit performing with the lions after a fire—it's a long story. So, then he started managing all the acts. That's how I learned all the things I showed you."

"You obviously think highly of your father. I suppose you miss him."

"Of course. Very much. Don't you think highly of your father?"

"I do. I mean, I respect him." His eyes darted towards the ground. "We just don't agree on much."

"Maybe today changed his mind about you and gator wrestling."

"Maybe a little. He still doesn't want me traveling with the fair and performing, but he's offered to let me go live with my uncle in Silver Springs."

"The one who builds canoes? I overheard your conversation this morning."

"Yeah, that's the one."

"You don't want to go?"

"I'm not sure. The only thing I know I want is to see you again; and if I go…"

There went my heart again, and my face flushed. James took hold of my hand and held it.

"We could write," I said in a quiet, almost sad tone.

"I guess." He looked disappointed.

"I know it's not the same, but you have to go where you can do what you love and be happy."

He stepped so close to me I could feel his breath escape his mouth. Then, he kissed me; keeping his lips pressed against mine for more than a brief moment before pulling away.

"You're lucky I'm the one who heard your commotion out here, ya know. Could've been my uncle out here with a gun instead of me with a kiss."

"It was worth the risk," he replied with an adorable grin.

It felt as if my heart skipped a few beats.

***

Not long after that night, James left for Silver Springs, but not without my address. A week later, I received a letter from Albert with a beautiful blue feather enclosed. Part of me felt excited by all the interest—two beaus who wanted to be near me. The other part of me felt ashamed in keeping each secret from the other. Only Lizzie could be my confidant, and I entrusted her with knowledge of my two love interests, and the turmoil of my emotions.

"You're really just friends with them both; so it's perfectly fine," Lizzie encouraged me one day while snapping green beans in the kitchen. "I mean, neither one is actually courtin' you."

"No, I suppose not. And, truthfully, what are the chances either one will come back here? Of course the thought of never seeing them again is terribly sad. I can't win! Either I feel bad for liking them both so much or I feel bad thinking they're lost to me forever."

"Gee whiz, Ruth, quit feelin' sorry for yourself, and enjoy the attention for a while. I wish two cute boys liked me! Heck, I'd settle for one right now."

I laughed at her sarcasm but she was right. I could always count on Lizzie to tell me what I needed to hear—no holding back.

"How many quarts of green beans are we gonna can?" I asked.

"As many as we can fill," Aunt Jane replied, as she walked into the kitchen with another bucket of beans.

"We should cook a big pot of 'em, too," added Lizzie. "With fatback. They'll be good with supper."

"Sounds good to me," I chimed-in.

"Alright. Set aside a pot full, but the rest we're canning and takin' to the cellar. Oh, and a few jars we'll take to Widow Smith. I need to check on her anyhow."

I sat in a rickety kitchen chair, leaning over a bucket of green beans, thinking about how different my life had become. Normally, I'd have been finishing up my dish-washing, and running after my father to check the safety latches on the animal cages or to observe a new routine the acrobats were rehearsing. So much change in such a short amount of time, it seemed.

A knock on the front door disrupted my thoughts. Aunt Jane went to see who it was, and we heard the muffled sounds of a brief conversation before the door closed.

"Helen!" Aunt Jane called out. I heard my mother walk into the living room, and my stomach turned. Lizzie and I glanced at each other, dropped the green beans we held in our hands, and ran into the other room.

Mother was holding a telegram. Her hands shook as she opened it.

"What is it?" I pleaded, desperate to know if something terrible had happened.

"It's your father. He's been wounded, and taken to a hospital in Belgium. It says the hospital will notify us of his condition when possible."

I could tell she was trying to keep a brave face.

"Alright. So, we know he was well enough to travel to a hospital. That's certainly a good thing," said Aunt Jane, attempting positivity.

"What do we do now? Can we contact the hospital?" I asked.

"I wouldn't begin to know how. I think all we can do is wait," she replied.

The four of us stood there just looking at each other; all thinking the same thing: waiting is a horrid and difficult task.

***

It was mid-September before we received any news on my father's condition. We were told his sight had been damaged by the flash from an explosion, but that was the extent of the information. We had no idea if he was completely blind, partially blind, or if he had the possibility to fully recover. The letter said he would be returned to the States in four to six weeks, and that we would be notified of his arrival. Once again, all we could do was wait.

***

October arrive and the temperature was in the seventies; a cool enough difference from the summer heat to feel like fall for people living in Florida. A week before Halloween, we were notified of my father's return. Uncle Ed went to pick him up from the train station. Mother had wanted to go; but not knowing his condition, it was agreed the more room in the cab of the truck, the better. She could greet him warmly when arrived at the house.

Lizzie and I made paper chains and hung them on the front porch with a big poster that read "welcome home." Instead of pumpkins and leaves, our house looked like we were prepared for the fourth of July. Even our neighbors joined-in, and had flags and banners festooning their porches and fences.

I heard Uncle Ed blast his horn, and ran onto the front porch; heart beating fast, stomach in knots, wondering what to expect. Mother stood beside me and held my hand; squeezing 'til it almost hurt. The truck stopped in front of the house, and the passenger door swung open. My father, looking regal in his dress uniform, stepped out; and at first, I didn't notice anything different about him. Then, I saw it. A bandage and patch over his right eye.

He stood tall and straight and waved at neighbors who called out to him. They had never even met him, but they knew where he had been and what he had been doing, and they admired him for it.

Mother ran to him, and hugged him tightly; tears flowed down both their faces. Everyone clapped, and Uncle Ed gave my father a hardy pat on the back. Suddenly, Father looked right at me.

"There's my girl," he said, smiling.

I was frozen. I wanted so badly to run to him, but my feet wouldn't move. My mouth wouldn't open. All I could do was stand there and cry. Father walked up the little path, up the two steps, and stood in front of me on the porch.

"Ruthie," he began; but I wrapped my arms around him tightly and sobbed into his chest before he could say another word.

***

We made a feast of a supper that night. Pork roast, potatoes, fresh baked rolls, and some of those green beans we had canned; not to mention both an apple and a pecan pie. Father commented more than once that he had eaten so much he might burst, but that didn't stop him from getting seconds or dessert.

After supper, Lizzie and I set to cleaning the kitchen while the adults sat by the radio and sipped coffee.

"Two of the doctors say the damage is permanent," Father told them. "But, a third doctor said he thought I could regain sight."

"I like the third doctor," commented Aunt Jane.

"So do I. He was younger, but more knowledgeable about recent treatments and research. I have his information, and I think I'll contact him next week."

"Right now you should simply rest-" Mother began before he interrupted.

"Helen, honey, all I have done for weeks is rest. There's only so much lying in bed a man can take. I can see well enough to work. Please, Ed, tell me there's something I can do."

Uncle Ed nodded. "Just so happens, I have a project or two."

I refilled coffee cups, and stopped by my father's chair. "What about the circus?" I asked, since no one else had.

The room fell silent, and my father looked down at his cup before looking me in the eye with his answer.

"There is no circus, Ruthie. Only Ringling is functioning right now. All of the small shows have disbanded; shows like ours. Everyone is scattered. Men are returning injured, like myself. We have to live differently now."

With a quick turn, I hurried back into the kitchen, set the coffee down, and ran out the back door. Lizzie followed after me.

"Is it so bad here?" she practically yelled at me.

"What?" I asked amid sobs.

"Is it so terrible living here, having your family together, staying in one house?"

"You wouldn't understand."

"No, I guess not," Lizzie huffed and stomped back into the house.

I wasn't sure why she was so mad at me. All I knew was I wanted my old life back. The realization that it would never be that way again made me sad. Why would my sadness make Lizzie mad?

Standing with my back to the house, I heard the back door squeak open and slam shut, and figured it was Lizzie coming to apologize. As the footsteps approached, I stifled my crying and wiped my nose with a handkerchief from my pocket.

"I know this has been difficult for you," I heard my father say, and turned around to see him.

"You're the one who had to go fight in a war. That's more difficult than canning beans and sweeping floors."

"You had to fight some battles, too, I hear. Guess I should teach you how to handle that whip."

I giggled through more tears. "Mother told you about that?"

"Yes. And about the Seminole boy you helped."

"Father, you should've seen him. He was pitiful."

Father let out a loud laugh. "I've seen some pitiful acts in my time. I didn't realize you were studying me so carefully."

"Always. Everything. You're the most brilliant man I know."

He hugged me tight and kissed my forehead. "Then follow my lead with this. Trust me. We can build a great new life outside of the circus. It won't be the same, but it can be good. And we'll be together; that's the most important thing."

"Yes, you're right, Daddy."

"And, you should talk to Lizzie."

"She got mad at me! Why on earth would she be mad at me?"

"Because she feels like you hate it here. Which would mean you hate-"

"Being with her; our times together," I said, realizing my error. "No, I don't! I cherish her! She's the best part of living here!"

"Then don't you think you should tell her that?" He asked.

"See. I told you you were smart."

***

I found Lizzie sitting on her bed, reading a book. "Lizzie?"

She looked up and glared at me; then returned to reading.

"I'm sorry, Lizzie. I haven't hated it here, honest. Having you to confide in and be adventurous with has been the best! Sure, I miss my friends from the circus, and I miss the life I knew. But, that doesn't mean I don't cherish here…or you."

"But, you wanted to go back to the circus instead of staying here," Lizzie spoke with her voice cracking and tears flowing.

I sat down on the edge of her bed. "Yes, but if we were going back, I'd be sad to leave here and I'd miss you."

"You just can't win," she said snidely.

I chuckled at her. "Guess not!"

We hugged, and she invited me to lie back and listen to her read this amazing story she had just begun, *Mary Poppins Opens the Door* by P.L. Travers.

***

A letter from James arrived filled with excitement. He had met the famous actor Johnny Weissmuller, who was filming another Tarzan movie there at Silver Springs. James wrote that he had been asked to show Mr. Weissmuller how he wrestled gators, and that he was given a lot of praise and five dollars! He couldn't believe he had so much money. His letter also said that he had ordered something from a catalog for me, and that I should receive it soon. I was overjoyed. I had never gotten anything from a catalog in my life!

***

The day the package arrived, I could hardly contain myself. I tore open the paper, but had to get my father to cut open the box with his pocket knife. Inside was a wood-handled, brush and mirror set with hand-painted pink flowers on their backs. I held them gently and admired their beauty.

Father whistled. "That boy spent some money on you. He must be smitten," he teased.

I was too happy to even be embarrassed. "I'm going to put these on the vanity right away."

Lizzie and I were now sharing a room; until my parents found a place of our own. Lizzie kept her things on the left side of the little vanity, and I kept mine on the right. The brush and mirror fit perfectly…right next to my Prince Albert tin full of feathers.

CHAPTER FOURTEEN

"I knew it! I knew there was a love triangle!"

"Oh, stop it," Ruth ordered. "Bragging is so unbecoming."

I couldn't help but laugh. "Alright, alright. There's some great stuff here. I jotted down notes so I'd remember to ask you about a few things."

"Like?"

"First, your interaction with James and his father. Weren't native Americans discriminated against back then?"

"Most definitely, but not much so by people of our standing. We were looked down upon with the same kind of disdain. And, my parents bringing me up in the circus world allowed us to befriend people of different ethnicities and cultures. My folks didn't have a racist bone in their bodies."

"Right. My ancestors were share-croppers, so they were considered 'white slaves.' They actually had a lot of African American friends because they were in similar circumstances."

Ruth nodded. "What else do you have questions about?"

"James meeting Johnny Weissmuller! I mean, how cool is that? The most famous Tarzan of the big screen."

"I still have his letter—the one in which he writes about that meeting. I'll find it for you."

"That would be awesome. And what about the Mary Poppins books? Did you and Lizzie read a lot of those?"

"All of them, I believe. Lizzie kept them. I'm sure they're around here somewhere."

"One last thing I want to ask you about, but it's not related to this story."

Ruth closed her eyes and leaned back in her chair. "Alright."

"Why did you request my articles about the police corruption case from the newspaper archives?"

"So you discovered it was me?"

"Not exactly, but now that you've confessed…"

"I see." She sat up straight and looked right at me. "I requested those articles because I wanted to re-trace how things happened, and to make sure you were the writer I wanted."

"What about that case made you want to choose me to write your story?"

"You see, one of those boys who was wrongfully charged, and convicted I might add, was my grandson, Jimmy."

"But, I thought the boys that were targeted were all Seminole…ohhhh." A light bulb went off in my head.

"I promise to give you the details of mine and James' story in the near future. For now, just know that you helped to set my grandson free, and your work showed him that there were still good people who cared about doing the right thing. Our family owes you a lot. I was hoping to reveal this later on, but you forced my hand—noticing the article I accidentally left out."

"You don't owe me anything. I was just doing what anyone would do.'

"No. Not anyone would jeopardize their job, possibly even their life, to expose corruption and vindicate a bunch of rowdy boys that society had given up on. No, sir. Not anyone would have done what you did. You and I both know those boys were guilty of a lot of things—fighting, vandalism. And because of that, they were easy targets for men in authority to use as pawns in their schemes."

"It wasn't just police, by the way. I don't know if you're aware, but the district attorney has built a case against some elected officials and the former police chief. She's asked myself and Lieutenant Ben Maupin—who worked the case as a detective—to help convince Seminole families to come forward with additional information. Our efforts so far haven't produced anything."

"Then I guess it's my turn to do the right thing. I have connections with people on the reservation through my late husband. James was highly esteemed…as an adult," she added with a grin. "His father's legacy allowed James to become an influential member of the tribe. Anyway, I will make some calls and see what I can do to help."

"Amazing how this all fits together," I said, thinking of her story and the case.

"We fit together…like that annoying Disney song…"

"It's a small world after all!" I began singing. "That's the one! But, yes, it is…a small world indeed."

***

As I was leaving Ruth's house, Katz called my cell to remind me I had a charity fundraising event to attend, and that he assigned a photographer to join me. Can't say I was particularly thrilled about any of this, but it was my job. I came to this area to do this kind of "fluff" work in order to escape the chaos of big city journalism—specifically the constant struggle with my editor who refused to believe my allegations in spite of the proof from my sources.

Then there was the slander thrown at me from the police chief, the threats from some of the corrupt cops—one of which actually pulled me over and gave me a bogus ticket. I paid the fine, and let it be. All this time I've been hiding out here, writing about socialites buying art and donating to worthy causes, avoiding forming friendships; all in an effort to escape and recover from that whole ordeal. It hadn't worked. I missed writing real stories. I missed feeling as though what I did had a purpose. I even missed being social…sometimes. Geez, I sounded like Ruth when she had her pity party. This was not a good sign.

I drove to the office and knocked on Katz's door. He waved me in; I shut the door behind me and didn't bother sitting down.

"I'm going to the fundraiser tonight, obviously, but…this is the last one." I informed him with resolution.

"You write about social events, Mike. This can't be your last one." He said as if I was just being flippant.

"It can if I'm no longer writing about social events."

Katz looked up from his desk and stared at me curiously. "Are you suggesting you want to write for real? As in actual pieces about news; stuff that matters—that sort of thing?"

"I am."

Katz leaned back in his chair with his hands behind his head and grinned. "I knew this day would come."

"A wise woman once told me that bragging is unbecoming."

"It's not bragging if it's true! I knew your writer instincts would kick back in, and you'd climb out of this pit you built yourself."

"Pit? That's a bit harsh."

"No, it's not. So, what are your plans exactly?"

I filled Katz in on the case being built, Ruth's connections with the Seminole tribe, and the effort to get witnesses to come forward. He was practically drooling over all the news-worthy content I was presenting.

"This could be huge. But, you need more resources to put this together. As much as I hate it, I should reach out to my connections at…"

"No. We may be a small publication, but we can handle this. Besides, there are a few guys over at the city paper that I don't trust—might be part of this scandal."

"This just keeps getting bigger…and better. I mean, it's terrible, but you know—for us it's great."

I chuckled. "Yeah, I know. Okay, so I'm off to get my tux…God help me."

"Hey, this is your swan song in the world of art and society. Make it special."

I rolled my eyes, and left his office; feeling better than I had in a long time.

***

Art from the Heart was the name of the fundraiser for an art therapy center. It was certainly a good cause; I liked the idea. Socialite schmoozing, however, was not something I enjoyed. Still, I made my best effort to look as though I fit in—hair in a bun, smoothed with actual product; classic black tux with skinny tie, kind of *Mad Men* inspired. All I needed to complete the look was a martini, but I don't like them.

"Look at you!" exclaimed Betty, the photographer Katz had assigned to this event.
"Am I a train wreck?"

"No, not at all! Very sexy, actually."

"I won't tell your husband you said that."

Betty laughed. "He's home watching the kids and cooking supper, and he'll give me a foot massage when I get home. His position is secure."

"A foot massage? Is your husband actually real? I mean, come to think of it, I've never seen him."

"I got the last good one. At least that's what my single friends say. Speaking of single friends…"

"Nope. Don't even go there. I'm not in dating mode right now."

She shook her head with disapproval, but to her credit, she didn't pressure me to go on a blind date. We perused the art displays and munched on hors d'oeuvres. I spoke with some of the therapists and the program director; using my smallest digital recorder to remain discreet. Betty snapped photos, and found most people were more than happy to pose for a publication.

"Will this be on your Facebook page, too?" asked one party patron.

"Possibly. I'll post as many pictures as I can. Check our page in the morning," Betty replied.

"Everyone wants their shot at fame," I whispered to Betty. She giggled, and moved on to the next group of lawyers, doctors, and retired Northerners who transplanted to the area—the typical kinds of people found at these events.

"Mr. Tallen," said a woman's voice from beside me; somewhat familiar.

I turned to see the D.A., Carolyn Nelson. She looked different from her pant suit office attire persona. She wore a navy sequined ball gown, and her hair in large curls that rested on her shoulders.

"I almost didn't recognize you," I admitted.

"I can say the same for you. Are you here as a patron or a writer?"

"Writer. This isn't my kind of party."

"Mine either. I'd prefer to be at home in my pajamas watching Netflix."

I had to laugh because I could relate. "So, what brings you here then?"

"I have an autistic son who has art therapy with that woman over there," she motioned with her hand, holding a glass of wine. "He loves it, and she is terrific with him."

"That's cool. So, could I ask you a few questions about your son's therapy? For an article?"

"Sure."

We spent about ten minutes discussing her son's diagnosis, and how art therapy had helped him to try new things and even develop better fine motor skills. I thanked her for her time, and she left to retreat to her pj's and another episode of *Stranger Things.* If this was my swan song, as Katz put it, it was certainly going to be a good one. Not that other charity events don't have worthy recipients, but this one in particular intrigued me. I decided I'd go online and make a donation when I got home.

***

Thursday morning, I found myself at 9th Bar, yet again, due to my intense craving for espresso.

"You should try breakfast sometime," Omar suggested.

"You mean something besides coffee?"

"Yes, besides coffee."

"Hmmm…maybe I should. How about the Bruce Lee?" I read the menu, "Ham, Havarti, egg and tomato on an English muffin…yep, that sounds good."

"One Bruce Lee, coming up!" Omar said with glee. It was like he'd won something.

While I waited, Ben called.

"Hey," I answered.

"Just had a warrant for your arrest come across my desk," Ben teased.

"Don't mess with me, man. I'm having Bruce Lee for breakfast."

"What?"

I realized it wasn't worth trying to explain. "Never mind. What's up?"

"Got a call at the station from a Seminole family last night. Their daughter actually took video of a conversation between the deputy mayor and a police officer discussing drug sales! She was hiding around the corner, and using her cell phone. Can you believe that? Talk about evidence!"

"Was it someone we talked to?"

"No, they said an old family friend convinced them to let their daughter come forward. I called the D.A., and she was meeting with them this morning to get the testimony and the video."

"That's intriguing. I hope that seals the deal for her case. And, I hope this family can stay protected."

"I'm already on that. I have some connections in that precinct—honest guys I know can be trusted."

"I hope you're right about that." I said.

"Gotta run, but thought you'd want to know."

"Yeah, thanks, buddy."

I hung up and dug into my Bruce Lee sandwich that just been placed in front of me. It was nice and hot; cheese melting down the sides. It was like a party for my taste buds. With the exception of the giant octopus painted on the wall next to me, I was in heaven.

***

Arriving at Ruth's ten minutes late, I apologized profusely.

"Oh, it's alright. I'm not going anywhere…yet."

"Before we get started, I want to thank you for speaking with people you know on the reservation. Apparently, a family came forward with some terrific evidence that should be the smoking gun, as they say."

"Marvelous. Glad I could be of service. Sometimes people just need reassurance, and a little voice of reason to get motivated towards the right thing."

"Agreed," I confirmed with a grin. "I'm curious, though. How exactly did you manage to get them to come forward? And, how did you stumble across someone with such an amazing piece of evidence?"

"A wise woman doesn't reveal all her secrets."

"That statement just doubled my curiosity."

"Your journalistic instincts must be kicking in. I'll share more information when it's the proper time."

"I've gotten to know you well enough that I'm fairly certain begging wouldn't get me anywhere."

"You're correct. I only say what I want to say."

"I have no doubt of that. So, what are you going to say today?"

"Well, I guess it's time we jump forward a bit in our story. But, not as far as you might think. I need to share something from 1944, and go from there."

"Start whenever you like. I'm just along for the ride," I teased.

"Then hold on; this ride is about to get bumpy," she quipped.

CHAPTER FIFTEEN

Mother and I had finished cleaning up the dishes from supper, and the three of us had gathered in the living room of our new house, listening to the radio when the news broke. June 6, 1944…a fire broke out during the matinee performance of the Ringling Brothers Circus…over a hundred and fifty people dead, over seven-hundred injured. It was a terrible disaster, and one with far-reaching devastation. Multiple members of families killed, young children who survived traumatized, and circus workers' livelihoods hanging in the balance.

The next day, we read in the paper about circus performers rescuing children, crewman slicing through the tent to make additional exits so people could escape, and others who jumped into action to save lives. An image on the front page showed the massive big top engulfed in flames. I saw it and my heart sank.

Father got on the phone and tried to make contact with as many of our circus family members as he could. The Baldocchi's were doing trapeze acts for another circus in Chicago; Arman and Cyrus were out west working as ranch hands; Donald and Hank were still with Albert and the elephants working for a different circus performing in Tennessee.

It was such a relief to hear that they were all safe. But, everyone shared a lingering concern—would this tragedy mark the beginning of the end for the circus?

Over the next month, Ringling Brothers managed to salvage their season by using arenas, stadiums and ballparks in place of their tent. Their train went from seventy-nine to sixty-seven cars just by eliminating the canvas and poles for the big top. Feeling safe in the new locations, circus-goers continued to buy up tickets for Ringling Brother shows. It was the small circuses, however, that suffered; unable to secure alternate venues, and having to continue their reliance on tents, made them seem vulnerable to another such disaster. Attendance at the smaller shows dwindled.

It wasn't long 'til member of our circus family began reaching out to my father in search of work or assistance. Some needed him as reference as to their work ethic and skills. Others were hoping he and Mr. Lewis would renew the show. Normando called because he had finally heard the news that Father was home from the War, and said he hoped to visit us one day.

***

Another month passed, and I answered the phone when it rang. "Clarke residence."

"Ruth? Is that you?" It was Albert. I nearly dropped the receiver.

"Albert? I've been hoping you would call! Wait, you're alright aren't you? Everything's ok isn't it?"

"I'm alright. Pricha...she got sick again, on a train car with other elephants. This time she didn't make it." I could hear the extreme sadness in his voice.

"Oh, Albert. I'm terribly sorry."

"The show isn't doing well either. We use a tent, and people...well..."

"They're scared. Father said it might happen this way."

"I don't suppose he's talked with Mr. Lewis."

"He has, actually, but nothing came of it. Mr. Lewis sold a lot of the gear and riggings, and with shows struggling right now—doesn't make sense to put a new one together."

"No, I suppose not. Sorry I haven't written in a few weeks. It's been difficult."

"That's alright, Albert. I understand."

Father came in from his job at the bottling company; the sight in his injured eye back at sixty percent.

"Who're you talking to?" Father asked.

I covered the phone with my Albert and whispered, "Albert, Father. Pricha passed away."

He motioned for me to hand him the phone.

"Albert, son, this is Mr. Lewis. So sorry to hear about Pricha."

The two of them talked about a half an hour. I left the room as a courtesy, but I was so curious as to what they were discussing; it was all I could do not to eavesdrop. Finally, my father called me into the kitchen where he sat at the table helping Mother peel apples.

"Sit down, Ruthie, and help us out. I'm in a hurry for some of your mother's apple pie."

I giggled, "Yes, Sir. Did you have a nice talk with Albert?"

"I did. We discussed Pricha's illness and passing, the poor attendance at the show he's been performing with, and then we made a decision."

"A decision?"

"Yes. Albert is coming here."

I dropped the knife and apple onto the table. I could feel all the blood rushing to my face. I quickly picked up the knife and began peeling again. Father laughed heartily.

"Ruth Ann, you can't fool me. You've been sweet on that boy for as long as anyone can remember."

Mother came to my rescue by changing the subject. "He'll be staying with your aunt and uncle and Lizzie since they have a spare room. I'd like you to help me make some new curtains for your Aunt Jane to show our gratitude for letting him stay."

"Yes, ma'am," I agreed, with a big grin that I could not remove from my own face, no matter how hard I tried. I was happy, and that was all there was to it.

***

Albert arrived a few weeks after that initial phone call, and began working at the bottling company with my father and uncle. Letters from James had come less frequently, and finally stopped altogether; I never even mentioned James to Albert. My focus was on this relationship. I was now seventeen, Albert was eighteen; and so with my parents' permission, we began dating.

Our first official date was to a dance held at the Rotary Club. As we entered, the band was playing "Swinging on a Star," the popular Bing Crosby song. I wore a green dress with ruffled sleeves and a belt at the waist. Albert wore a suit and tie, and it was the first time I had ever seen him so dressed up. He had brought me a wrist corsage of pink carnations; and I thought it was the most beautiful thing I had ever seen.

We didn't dance much as neither one of us were confident in our dancing skills. Afterwards, we went with a group of friends to a local diner; and for dessert we shared a chocolate malt. I knew right then and there, Albert was the one; and he felt the same way about me. He also knew, however, that he needed a better income to support a wife and family. So, he set a plan into motion to achieve certain goals before he'd even propose. I thought he was just dragging his feet.

***

Three years passed, and I was growing impatient; having not received a proposal yet. Albert, on the other hand, had worked hard and risen in the company with two promotions and a considerable pay raise. Unbeknownst to me, he had also procured a modest home just a block away from my parents and two blocks from Aunt Jane, Uncle Ed and Lizzie.

One evening we had planned to see a movie—*The Ghost and Mrs. Muir*, followed by dinner. Throughout the movie, Albert jostled his legs and fidgeted in his seat; annoying me to no end. By the time the movie ended, I was in a foul mood and ready to head home. He managed to convince me to go on to dinner; informing me that we had friends meeting us there. Instead of driving to a local restaurant, Albert turned down a residential road.

"Where are we going? This isn't the way to the diner."

"I know. I have a surprise first."

At first my heart skipped, and I felt the joy of anticipation—could he finally be proposing? But, then my inner skeptic kicked-in, and I let myself feel bothered that I didn't know what was going on, and he was being so secretive.

He pulled the car—a black, 1942 Ford he bought used after his first promotion—into a driveway by a little white cottage with a front porch just big enough for a couple of chairs. It was sweet, and I loved it immediately.

"Who's house is this?" I asked, thinking we were visiting someone he knew.

"It's ours," he replied.

I stared at him in disbelief. He got down on one knee, right there in that driveway, and asked me to marry him. Some girls get offered a ring; I got offered a house.

***

Two months after he proposed, we were married on a hot July afternoon at the little Baptist church I had attended since arriving in Fort Lauderdale. Lizzie was my maid of honor, and wore a pale yellow dress with a navy blue sash. About thirty guests, including my family and Albert's mother and sisters, were in attendance. And, one other special guest who surprised us; thanks to my father.

As I walked down the aisle towards my husband-to-be, I noticed the cheery, familiar face and larger-than-life presence of Normando standing within the pews. He was dressed in a navy suit—the most conservative thing I had ever seen him wear—with a yellow carnation in his lapel. I noticed he took a handkerchief from his pocket to wipe tears from his eyes as I passed by.

The ceremony was lovely; concluding with applause and cheers from our loved ones. Mother had arranged a marvelous reception with a cake and punch; where we greeted our guests. I gave Normando the biggest hug I could manage.

"I can't believe my precious girl is all grown up," he told me while trying not to cry.

"You'll have to come over for tea, and let me be hostess. But, you're still responsible for providing the words of wisdom."

He nodded the affirmative, and kissed my forehead.

We ran from the church to Albert's old Ford amidst a shower of rice, and headed off for a short honeymoon in our own house. Instead of spending money on travel and a hotel; we opted to buy furnishings and curtains for our little home.

"Are you sure about this?" Albert asked me as I got out of the car.

"Sure about what?"

"Staying here for our honeymoon. I'll drive to the beach right now if you'd rather…"

"Albert, darling, this is exactly where I want to be."

He lifted me up and carried me up the two steps onto the porch, and through the threshold. I rewarded him with a lingering kiss. Then, the honeymoon began.

***

Ten months later, we welcomed our first child; a son whom we named John Walter Martinelli—his middle name after my father. Two years after his birth, came our second son, William Edward Martinelli—his middle name after my uncle. Albert had insisted we not use any names from his family; especially not his father's side. He had embraced my family as his own, and only kept in touch with his mother, sisters and brothers through letters. Albert's issues with his own father caused him to determine not to repeat them. He was attentive and affectionate with our boys.

John and Billy followed after their father in almost every way. They had his dark hair and slender build; and a thirst for adventure and acrobatics. One day, when they were nine and seven years old, I peered out the kitchen window to see the two of them hanging from a tree limb and attempting to swing themselves high enough to flip in the air before landing on the ground. Before I could get outside, they each tried this feat—John landed safely, but Billy fell on his arm and broke it. When we got home from the doctor, I had initially wanted to punish them.

"Do you know the tricks I tried when we were growing up? You don't think I landed all those flips and somersaults the first time, do you?"

"No, of course not," I replied. "But, at least you had areas to practice that were safer than a tree in a backyard. And you had people to spot you."

That weekend, Albert put an old crib mattress under the tree, and spent hours showing the boys how to flip and how to fall safely and correctly.

***

Albert and I worked to build a loving home for our family. It was true devastation when in 1962, at the age of thirty-six, Albert died from a sudden heart attack. I lost my husband, my soulmate, my best friend, my partner...it was as if part of me had been cut away, and was gone forever.

For the first time in my life I felt vulnerable, frightened, and hopeless. Even in dark times, when my father was sent to war, for example; I kept a sense of hope—there was always a glimmer of light. But, Albert's passing was unlike anything I had ever experienced. The weight of his loss buried me.

The boys were twelve and fourteen; stages in life when a boy needs his father desperately. But, Albert was gone, and I was unavailable; hidden away in my bed and laden with grief. Lizzie had married just a couple of years after I had—a fine man named Thomas, and they had two children; a son and a daughter.

Eight months had passed, and I was still barely attending to my own hygiene. Sending the boys to get TV dinners from the store; essentially ignoring everyone and everything but my own misery. Lizzie and Thomas, having been kept well informed by my oldest son John, showed up one summer and got to work. They cleaned the house, fixed meals, took their children and mine on outings, and tried their best to get me back on my feet.

Finally, at the end of their two-week stay, Lizzie approached me with a proposition. "Ruth, sit up and look at me. I have something to say."

I sat up in my bed, still in my nightgown at one in the afternoon.

"We have tried everything, and I'm at my wit's end with you," Lizzie scolded me.

"Wit's end? With me?" I was appalled.

"Yes! With you! You have two young men who need their mother. Your finances are in shambles, and you'll be homeless within two months—if it even takes that long."

"I'm mourning for my Albert!"

"No! No, you're not! You're wallowing in self-pity. I know you miss him. I know it's a terrible loss. But, you have responsibilities to yourself and to your children. You need to get up, get dressed, and get to work!"

"How dare you! You don't know what it's like to lose someone you love…"

"You're about to lose more than just Albert. These boys can't take it here anymore. They need parenting."

"They're practically grown. They'll be fine."

"No, Ruth. They are still children, and they need guidance, security. For Pete's sake, Ruth, they need meals and help with homework—you're not even doing that!"

"I'm suffering!" I argued.

"And you're adding to their suffering! This isn't just about you! Why, Ruth Ann, if I had your father's whip, I'd use it on you!"

"Get out!" I screamed at the top of my lungs.

"I am! And I'm taking John and Billy with me!" Ruth had planned on merely suggesting she and Thomas take the boys for a while, but my stubbornness led to them taking them while I laid in bed crying and screaming my hatred at Lizzie.

***

It took me two more months, an eviction notice, and the realization that my sons weren't even calling me on the phone anymore to realize I had to change things. I finally showered, got dressed, and decided to take some cash I had hidden away and get my hair done so I'd look more presentable and maybe even feel better. I hadn't been to a hair salon in over a year, and had never been to the one I found while driving around downtown.

The hairdresser took me back to wash my hair; and I sat down, I glanced at the row of hairdryers to see an older man sitting under a dryer, reading a magazine. He looked strangely familiar, but I figured I was imagining things. I leaned back to have my hair washed, and it suddenly occurred to me that I had not imagined anything—I knew exactly who that man was! I stopped the hairdresser's hands as she was applying shampoo, sat straight up, and yelled across the room. "Normando?!"

The man dropped his magazine, looked right at me, and his jaw dropped open.

"Ruth?" He pulled the hair dryer up off his head, and dragged his chair over by me.

We hugged, and I let the hairdresser do a quick wash before we began talking; assuring her I'd let her cut and style my hair after my reunion with an old friend.

"I can't believe it's you—you're here, of all places!" I kept staring at his face in amazement. He was in his seventies now, but not looking much different except for the all-white hair and deeper creases near his eyes.

"I came out here hoping to find you. Hated losing touch with you after your parents moved further south, and I moved further north. Last I heard, you and Albert had two young boys."

I sighed, and fought back tears. "Not so young anymore. Fourteen and twelve."

"My, my! Time surely does fly. I bet Albert has them out on adventures while you're here getting spruced-up."

"I'm afraid not. Albert…he's passed. Heart attack."

Normando just shook his head, and hugged me tight. "Words can't express," he whispered.

"Now, you said you came to find me. Is that true?"

"Yes, it is. My only cousin passed away last year, and I found myself in need of family. I'm retired, and fortunately I saved over the years so I'm living comfortably. I just need-"

"Connection."

"Yes, that's it. People to connect with; and maybe someone to share a cup of tea and conversation."

"Just so happens, I'm available for teas and conversations," I said with a laugh; my first laugh since Albert died.

***

A week later, just before school was to start, my boys returned home and met "Uncle Norman." He wasn't the kind of man Albert had been—masculine, adventurous, physically fit and athletic. But, Normando (as I still affectionately called him) taught the boys manners, respect for others who were different from them, and the importance of self-confidence.

A few times, the boys' friends would tease them or poke fun at their Uncle Norman, but my sons stood up for their loved one and defended him fiercely.

One day, while at the grocery store altogether, some older boys called Normando crude names; laughing and pointing, and causing a scene.

John and Billy walked up to the boys, their arms crossed over their chests.

"You need to apologize," John demanded.

"Yeah? I think you need to apologize for us having to see your creepy little family out here in public," taunted one of the gang of juvenile delinquents.

"Ya'll are a bunch of freaks...like circus freaks!" said another.

"Yes, we are," replied Billy.

The older boys laughed. "Hear that? He admits it!"

"We come from a long line of circus performers, actually. And, we're very proud of our heritage," added John.

"In fact, our grandfather, was a renowned performer," said Billy to a confused and awe-struck group of boys.

"Oh, really?" was the only comeback one of the bullies could offer.

"Yes, really. Want to know what act he performed?" Billy asked, winking at John. At this point, I knew they had something up their sleeves.

"He was the lion tamer," John said matter-of-factly, pulling my father's whip from his back pant pocket and cracking it across the tile floor. The people standing nearby gasped, the store manager came charging towards us—mad as a hornet, but the bullies ran off embarrassed. I grabbed the boys and Normando, and we left in a hurry; leaving my cart of groceries sitting mid-aisle. We were a block down the road before anyone said anything.

"John Walter," I began.

"Yes, ma'am," he replied sheepishly.

"Where did you get that, and what made you think to use it in such a manner?"

"It was in a box of stuff in the garage, and...um...well, Uncle Norman told us how you used it to defend cousin Lizzie, so-"

We stopped at a stop sign, and I looked over at Normando in the passenger seat. He just smiled and shrugged, and we both burst out laughing.

"Are they laughing because it's funny or is it more like when the villain on TV announces his evil plan?" Billy whispered to John.

"I'm not sure," John confessed.

Normando and I just laughed even harder, and let the boys squirm with fear all the way home.

CHAPTER SIXTEEN

"**So, you married** Albert, your childhood sweetheart. Shame he had to give up performing to bottle soda, though."

"I suppose it is. But, he had a family to support; and circus jobs were so few, the competition was incredible."

"Job security and opportunities for promotion are definitely a plus. He did the right thing."

"That he did," Ruth agreed with a smile.

"And I love that Normando came back into your life. How awesome is that? Although I need to remember to stay on your good side. That whip keeps making appearances…"

Ruth cackled. "Yes, it does! Lizzie even used it once to scare away a would-be thief! I have it tucked away in a safe deposit box for future generations. Probably time I got it out and shared it."

"If you do, you've gotta give me a call so I can check it out," I pleaded.

"Of course. Well, I'm afraid I'll be leaving for home the end of this week. If we can squeeze in one more meeting, I think I can finish things up."

I responded with a sigh and a sad expression on my face. "I won't know what to do with myself without our visits. I'll miss you terribly."

"You'll have writing to keep you busy and keep your mind occupied. But, I'll miss you, too."

I packed up my recorder, and like a quick flip of a switch, something occurred to me.

"Ruth, if you married Albert; then how is it your grandson is part Seminole? And you said James' legacy gave you connections on the reservation."

"That story is for next time. Patience, Michael…it's a virtue."

"Do I look like the virtuous type?"

"No, but in my experience, virtuous people rarely do."

***

A few days later, Ben called and asked to come over after work. So, I put in some time at the office, swung by Nature's Food Patch Café for a spinach feta quiche and apple crisp, and got home in time to tidy the place up before Ben arrived.

It was nearly eight-o'clock when I heard his car pull in the driveway. I opened the front door and left it while I ran to the kitchen to remove the apple crisp from the oven where it was warming.

"You really shouldn't leave your front door standing wide open. It invites unsavory characters to just walk right in," Ben joked.

"I see what you mean," I fired back. "Next time I'll be more careful."

Ben sat on my thrift store sofa, and commented how it brought back memories. I offered him quiche and a glass of wine; both of which he accepted, and we sat and ate off the coffee table like a couple of teenagers.

"So, are you ready to hear the whole sordid story?" Ben asked, still chewing a bite of quiche.

"Dude, I'm a journalist…I'm always ready for a story."

"Alright then. First, the big news: the deputy mayor and former police chief were both arrested today."

"That was fast."

"The D.A. called in every favor she had to get things done quickly. And, I guess the mayor is trying to get out in front of this thing. So, he cooperated, and is having a press conference in the morning to spin it in his favor."

"Of course."

"Turns out, the deputy mayor has been overseeing a big drug ring, and he solicited the chief to get officers out there arresting the competition— namely, a Seminole gang. But, since they didn't know exactly who was in the gang, they took to arresting any Seminole youth they came across. Then, with bonuses getting paid out, cops started planting evidence so they could say they arrested a Seminole gang drug dealer, and, well…you get the idea."

"Holy crap. So, this thing is huge!"

"Yeah, and we don't even know how many officers were involved. Internal affairs will be doing a massive investigation, looking at arrests over the last five or six years. It could go on for some time."

We both took long sips of wine.

"I can't believe I was so worried over nothing. I mean, really, other than maybe having to testify again; this hasn't affected me much," I admitted.

"Yes, well…once you give a deposition, that could change. These guys have connections."

"Thanks," I said sarcastically, and feeling uneasy again.

"So, did you ever find out how your old lady storyteller is involved?"

"Not completely. All I know is that her grandson Jimmy was arrested and had drugs planted on him. You remember him from the original case?"

"Yeah. Jimmy was short and had this floppy hair…"

"Floppy hair?"

"You know, floppy...hung over his eye on one side," Ben said, trying to show me what he meant with his hand over his forehead.

"O.k. I remember him. Anyway, that's Ruth's grandson. But, as far as how she has any pull on the reservation, I'm not completely sure. She just said that she picked me to write her life story because of the articles I wrote revealing the corruption of the police force," I said with a shrug.

"Is it good? Her life story, I mean. Could you make a book out of it or something?"

"Maybe. I'm not really that kind of writer."

"Eh, you could do it. I bet by this time next year, you're on the New York Times bestseller list."

I let out a boisterous laugh. "That, my friend, is the funniest thing I've heard in ages."

***

Following my journalist instincts, as Ruth called it, I got an early start and rode Bonnie to the Seminole reservation. It was a nice ride; quiet except for Switchfoot's *Beautiful Letdown* album blasting through my earbuds. Most of the traffic headed for the casino or other tourist traps. I went into the residential areas, flashing my press credentials as needed to get directions or other information. Obvious signs of poverty and drunken behavior were scattered about; boarded-up windows, overgrown lawns of repossessed houses, broken glass in the streets.

"Hey, fellas," I called out to a group of teenage boys huddled around an '89 Mustang fox body, faded red with a white soft top that had seen better days.

"You lost?" One of them asked.

"Not exactly," I held up my press ID. "I'm hoping to find someone who likes to talk."

The boys all laughed. "Talk or snitch?" asked one of the group, apparently the leader, of sorts.

"Just talk. I write for the paper, and a few years ago I helped put some dirty cops away. The case is open again, and…"

"You the guy who wrote about Jimmy?"

"Yeah, that's me. His grandmother Ruth is a friend of mine."

The group leader walked closer to me; calling over his shoulder for the others to "go get some cigs or somethin'."

"Does this mean you're willing to talk, or should I fire up Bonnie here and make a quick getaway?"

"Nah, man, you're cool. We're just having a conversation," he assured me.

"So, you know Jimmy. Know anything about this drug war with the police?"

"Man, it's all messed up. It's…what's that word when everyone's against one group, but another group gets a pass?"

"Bias?"

"Yeah, that's it! There's bias! Those fellas sellin' drugs for the politician—they call him the Commander—they get away with everything. No hassle, no nothin'. Our guys get picked up for jay-walkin', man. That ain't even worth breakin' out the cuffs, ya know? But, they say you tried to run or start a fight, and so they had to handcuff you. Next thing you know, there's drugs in your back pocket."

"Sounds like you're speaking from experience."

"This is just…what's that word?"

"Hypothetical?"

"Yeah, that's it."

"So, hypothetically, how would an old woman like my friend Ruth convince people that live here on the reservation to come forward with information?"

"Well, man…she's got cred."

"Like street cred?"

"Better. She's got res cred. She's the widow of James Cypress, a respected leader. The story is, she taught him how to make money puttin' on a gator wrestling show, and years later they met again and fell in love, and came to the reservation to help the tribe. It's almost like a legend or somethin'. After he died, she kept on helping our tribe to get better education and services…like shrinks and stuff."

"Like psychologists…for mental health?"

"Yeah, like that. She did fundraising and schmoozed with high society types to get things we needed here."

"So she's well-liked; respected."

"Man, I once got mad because she had worked to pass some rules about us having to stay in school—I don't remember exactly. What I do remember is that I called her an old bag, and my grandma hit me so hard…"

I chuckled. "So, if she asked a family to tell the D.A. what they knew, they'd do it."

He paused for a moment. "I don't think they'd do it just because she asked. But, they'd listen to her, and think on it. Without her asking, there'd be no chance at all."

I thanked the kid for the info and was on my way.

***

My next stop for the day was my editor's office. Katz was waiting for me to bring him something he could headline.

His door was open, so I leaned in, "Just got back from the reservation, and-"

"Get in here! Close the door!"

I did as I was commanded. He took off his reading glasses, and set his papers aside.

"Go on—tell me everything," he instructed.

"Well, I think I've got enough to put together a solid story. I can quote a source, but they're confidential."

"Aren't they always," said Katz, oozing sarcasm.

"Still, it's reliable information and it confirms what I know from the D.A. Plus, there's an interesting angle in regards to Ruth, her grandson, and her influence with the Seminole tribe."

Katz perked up, and leaned forward on his desk. "I'm all ears."

***

That night, around three in the morning, I awoke from a sound sleep to the neighbor's dog barking. Lots of people have neighbors with dogs who bark at raccoons or the wind or whatever. But, my neighbor's dog rarely barked—something for which I was deeply grateful. However, when it's the middle of the night and you hear the dog bark—well, it's rather unsettling.

I switched on the lamp on my nightstand, and walked into the living room. When I reached the kitchen and turned on the light, a crashing sound came from outside. Grabbing the baseball bat I kept by the front door, I turned on the porch light, and stepped outside. One step, and I felt the squish of my door mat soaked in urine. The smell was strong, too. And, unfortunately, I was barefoot. So, some kids thought they were being funny, I figured—until I turned around. My front door was dripping with bright red paint, a butcher knife wedged into it for an added effect. This felt more ominous than some middle-schoolers peeing on a rug in response to a double-dog dare.

I walked further out, to my driveway, and saw Bonnie on her side. I'd have to check her out in the light to assess the damage; so I decided to roll her into my living room where she'd be safe until morning.

After locking all the doors and scrubbing my feet with Ajax, I fell back into bed; only to toss and turn and sleep ten minutes at a time until my alarm went off. My thoughts volleyed back and forth between coincidental prank, or warning about my involvement in this corruption case.
Somehow I blamed Ben for suggesting retaliation could still come. If he just hadn't said it.

***

"Lieutenant Maupin," Ben answered.

"I'd like to report a crime," I said, holding the phone with my shoulder while I scrubbed a quart of fake blood off my front door.

"Mike? I hope for your sake you're kidding. You don't live in my jurisdiction."

"I know you can't do anything about it, but no, I'm not kidding. My front door was covered in fake blood with a butcher knife sticking out of it; and Bonnie was knocked over when they tried to cut her brake lines."

"What? Seriously? Oh, man…this isn't good."

"My guess is that I spooked them when I turned on the light, so they quit trying to cut the lines, knocked over the bike, and ran off. Oh, they also peed on my welcome mat."

"They did what? So, maybe this is just a prank?"

"Seems awfully coincidental…"

"I was trying to be optimistic. Even with the pee thing, I don't think is random hoodlums causing trouble."

"Me neither," I sighed and stopped scrubbing the door. "And, I haven't even given my deposition yet."

***

It was time for my final meeting with Ruth to get the rest of her story. Still undecided about how I'd proceed with publishing this biographical tale, I had scribbled notes on a legal pad that only slightly resembled an outline. One thing was certain…no cheesy lists.

I had skipped breakfast, and would have given anything to be offered biscuits and tomato gravy; so Ruth's offer of a store-bought blueberry muffin was a bit of a letdown, but it kept my stomach from growling.

"Alright, so my inquisitive journalistic mind has figured some things out," I said to Ruth, peaking her interest.

"Do tell."

"Obviously, after Albert passed, you met up with James again, married and had at least one child; considering you have a grandson who was part Seminole. And, a little birdie told me that you gained a lot of influence on the reservation by being involved in charitable works and supporting James' efforts to improve life for his tribe."

"Why you're a bonafide Sherlock," she quipped.

"Ha. Ha. I know it's 'elementary,' but I've been writing about what designer dress the governor's wife wore to such-and-such art exhibit for the past two years. I'm rusty."

"Couldn't you have found countless details of my life online? I hear those Google searches are all the rage." Ruth was on a roll.

"Your sarcasm is in overdrive this morning! Yes, I could have done an online search, but I didn't because I wanted to hear your story from you—not from birth records and news articles."

"I appreciate that. I apologize for giving you a hard time."

"I secretly like it," I admitted.

"I know," she said with a chuckle.

"And, then there's the fact that I'm caught up in this corruption case again. Someone doesn't like my involvement, and they let me know it."

"What happened?" she asked, sounding worried. I explained the vandalism, and hoped I didn't make it out to be worse than it was.

"This is troublesome," she said, wringing her hands.

"Maybe I should borrow that whip," I teased, trying to lighten things up.

Ruth gave me an annoyed look. "I'm afraid we can't whip our way out of this one. Have you spoken to the police?"

"Not sure that's a good idea since there's a possibility one of them is involved."

"What about the district attorney? Is there anything she can do?"

"Doubtful. Besides, she has her hands full, and may be undergoing some attacks herself. I'm just not going to respond—not let them know they rattled me. It could still turn out to be nothing but kids."

"For once I am hoping there's a group of rowdy kids getting into mischief."

"Speaking of which, you left off with your sons causing some mischief in the grocery store."

"Yes, I did. But, I'm assuming you want less stories of their childhood antics, and more about my marriage to James."

"You assumed correctly!"

"Well, then...let's move along to 1964, two years after Albert died..."

CHAPTER SEVENTEEN

Both John and Billy played high school baseball. John was in his junior year, playing short stop; and Billy, being a sophomore, had just made the team as an outfielder. They were both athletic like their father—fast, agile. That particular year, their team, the blue and white Flying L's, went to the regional tournament.

Normando couldn't make the trip. By this time, his health was declining; so he stayed home and napped in his recliner. There I was, with a picnic lunch for three, a cushion to sit on, an umbrella for shade—all spread out in the stands to cheer on my boys. The other team was brand new school, North Marion High; the Colts. This was their first year in existence; so it was incredibly impressive for them to have made it to the tournament. Some of the parents of the Colts' team began arriving, and joined me in the stands.

The game began, and the Colts were up to bat first; meaning my boys were at short stop and in the outfield. A base hit went right to John, and his response was so quick getting the ball to first, it was an easy out. I cheered, and noticed only a handful of others cheered with me. The stands were mostly filled with parents and classmates of the other team. This didn't deter me in the slightest. The following batter struck out, and I cheered again. When the third batter for the Colts stepped up to the plate, I knew we were in trouble. He was a stocky Native American boy with big arms, and the crowd hushed when he stepped to the plate. The pitch was thrown; and with what looked like an effortless swing, the ball was hit up and over the fence—a homerun.

The stands rocked with cheers and the stomping of feet. I was annoyed until I heard a familiar sound. The cheers continued while the boy ran the bases, and I listened closely to better discern the voice I heard. Could it be?

I tried to scan the crowd, and pinpoint the origin of this eerily-familiar voice, but it was virtually impossible. Unfortunately for my sons and their team, the Colts were consistently scoring against the Flying L's. Fortunately for me, this meant the other spectators were cheering often, and I could maybe— just maybe—locate this person.

In the fourth inning, there was a questionable call at home plate, and the parents from the other team started complaining. That's when I heard him.

"Settle down, everyone. The umpire has final say, and we must respect his decision."

Memories of the conversation I overheard between Mr. Cypress and James flooded my mind. Mr. Cypress had a voice that commanded attention. But, something was different…besides, he would be so old now.

I had to know. I stood up and looked across the stands 'til I saw him, and I knew. James Cypress was standing on the other end, talking to the people around him.

"We're ahead by five. This out at home won't hurt us," I heard him say.

"Which kid is yours?" asked a gentleman seated behind James.

"None of 'em. That's my nephew," he pointed. "The one who was just called out at home."

Everyone laughed, and the mood lightened. I resolved to speak with him after the game; just to be sure.

***

Sure enough, the Colts beat the Flying L's 11 to 5, and my boys' time at the tournament had ended. They gathered their gear with slumped shoulders and sad faces, and we trekked toward the parking lot. As we passed the stands, I saw James standing off to the side, eating a hot dog.

"Boys, go on to the car. I'll be there in a minute," I instructed, handing Billy the keys.

With shaky knees, I walked up to this man I thought I knew, and spoke. "Excuse me...um...James?"

He looked up, and his eyes widened. He swallowed hard. "Ruth?"

"It's been so long; I wasn't sure. Honestly, when I heard your voice earlier, I thought you were your father!"

He grinned because he knew he sounded just like him now. "I..I can't believe it's you! What brings you here?"

"My boys. John and Billy play for the Flying L's."

"Oh! Oh, sorry about the game. Tough loss."

"Yes, well, they're resilient. I heard you say your nephew played?"

"Yeah, my middle sister's son. His father was killed tragically a few years ago; so I try to be around—go to games and such."

"That's good of you. Boys need a father-figure when one isn't available. Believe it or not, Normando has been around for my boys."

"The Great Normando? Really? Wait, so that means..."

"My husband, Albert, passed away."

"I'm so sorry, Ruth. Truly."

We chatted a few minutes more, and I was surprised to discover James had never married. He had returned the reservation at the age of twenty-two, and worked alongside his father. Before we could go any further in our conversation, I heard the honking of my car horn, and saw the boys waving their arms in desperation.

"I'd better go."

"Wait. Please," he took out his wallet and pulled from it a business card. "Would you write your number down for me? I'd love to give you a call and catch up."

I couldn't help but smile, and write my number before leaving.

"Who was that?" asked John.

"An old friend."

"How old?" asked Billy.

"After the circus days," I replied. "When we went to live with Aunt Jane, Uncle Ed and Lizzie."

"We'll have to ask Aunt Lizzie about this," John teased, talking to Billy.

"Oh no, you don't. You mind your own business!" I demanded.

The boys laughed, and John winked at Billy. I knew Lizzie would tell them all about James. I'd have to call her before they did.

***

Over the next two weeks, James and I talked on the phone every other night. We revisited our memories of his gator wrestling sideshow; and he shared details of his life at Silver Springs with his uncle.

"Uncle Charlie's canoes were works of art. He was such a skilled craftsman. Collectors still seek them out! The whole village was a great experience," James said proudly. "Father thought that putting our culture on display was an insult, but over the years, I managed to convince him it was an opportunity—not just for income, but for education. When people see how civilized and skilled a people we are; they have less reason for racism and hate."

"I love your passion for your people, James. Your father's legacy lives through you."

"There's still so much to be done. Life on the reservation is hard; so much poverty, alcoholism, lack of education."

"I wish there was some way I could help."

"There is."

"Well, tell me! What can I do?"

"Marry me."

"What?"

"Marry me, Ruth. Be my wife, my helpmate."

"I'll have to call you back," I replied quickly, and hung up the phone.

Three weeks later, we eloped at the courthouse. Normando, John and Billy were our witnesses. We honeymooned for one night at a local hotel, and had a party that weekend with James' sisters and their families.

***

Even though I was nearing forty, bearing children came easily for me. James and I had a son, James, Jr., born in '66; and a daughter came along a year later, Helen Elizabeth.

Helen was our biggest challenge; especially for me. She was fiercely independent, headstrong, and a lot like myself. Parenting boys who were like their father was easy. Parenting a daughter like oneself is near impossible. We butted heads, and sometimes I was the meanest mother in the whole world—her words, not mine. But, through it all, she graduated high school Valedictorian and graduated college with a degree in Social Sciences before she married and started a family.

We lived off the reservation in a nearby subdivision. But, all of our work was Seminole tribe-related. Our children spent countless hours in our offices, at community events, and at tribal festivities. Helen met her husband, a young Seminole man with passion like James, while working a fundraiser to build a new elementary school. They dated three years while she was in college, and was married two years before Jimmy came along.

Much like his mother, and his grandmother, I suppose; Jimmy was stubborn and difficult to parent. Only he didn't channel his energy into his education or even a hobby—he got into trouble. It started with small acts of vandalism that he and his buddies thought were funny. Things escalated when he served as the look-out while another kid stole money from a store. The money was being collected for a charity. Jimmy felt remorse, and tried to distance himself from that circle of friends.

But, one night, he went out with the same mischief-makers, off the reservation. They attended a party, but left early because of an argument over some girls. While walking down the street to their cars, a police car pulled up along the curb.

"Where ya boys headed?" asked the officer.

"We're just leaving," one of the boys replied.

"You're walkin' awfully fast. In a hurry?"

"No, sir," replied Jimmy. "The party was a bust, so we'll be going back to the res."

As soon as the reservation was mentioned, the officer called for back-up over his radio, and got out of his car.

"You need to get down on the ground—all of you!"

Two of the boys ran while Jimmy and two others got on the ground as they were told. While the officer patted them down, he placed small bags of drugs in their pockets. More officers arrived, and found the drugs. The boys were all arrested. Jimmy tried to convince them the drugs were planted, but of course, no one would believe him.

***

Our family rallied around Jimmy; we believed him, and we wanted to prove his innocence. But, while Jimmy was preparing for his court date, we got the news that James had stage four cancer. It was all so overwhelming, and at that point, Jimmy wanted to make a plea deal just to get it all over with. The same day he told me he wanted to give up proving his innocence was the same day an article came out in the newspaper: *Corrupt Cops Plant Evidence on Seminole Youth*. Jimmy found hope again. A journalist with a penchant for investigation had discovered witnesses and other victims who knew about the schemes of the police chief and some of his officers. It took six or seven articles over a period of months for anyone to take the allegations seriously. The biggest break came when the witnesses agreed to step out of the shadow of anonymity and into the light of testifying in court.

Jimmy's name was cleared just three days before James passed away. After the funeral, I sat Jimmy down and had a heart-to-heart.

"Your father and grandfather have great legacies they leave with you. The Seminole people have a strong heritage…one of warriors and survivors. But, I have a legacy to leave you, too. I learned at a young age that regardless of what other people thought, I could do anything I set my mind to do. We each have the freedom to be ourselves, and as for everyone else; well, they can like it or lump it. I must be true to myself, and I must stand for the things that are right. And, when I come across someone who is struggling to be themselves, and can't seem to stand up on their own feet; then it's my duty to stand for them, and lead them to find their confidence. I didn't have a tribe, but I had an extended family. I had people who cared, people who invested in me; and I pass their wisdom on to you. You have courage running through your veins. Use it for good. Are you understanding what I'm telling you?"

"Yes, ma'am. I value your wisdom, grandmother. I do. And, I value the heritage I have from you; not just from the tribe."

"Well, I may not have ancestors who were great warriors or chiefs, but I am the lion tamer's daughter…and that's good enough for me."

CHAPTER EIGHTEEN

I stopped the recorder, and leaned back in my chair with a contented sigh. "This feels like an ending," I said ruefully.

"Only temporary. You're a writer…think of today not as a period, but as a semicolon—a pause before we continue."

"You're saying there's more?"

"Of course there's more! Not only are there more stories from my past, but I'm not dead yet…there's more stories to come!"

I had to laugh. "You may even use that whip again!"

Now Ruth laughed. "You never know. I do like to surprise people. Speaking of surprising people; I have a little something for you."

Ruth picked up an envelope from atop the bed, and handed it to me. It had yellowed with age, but the handwriting was still discernable. Addressed to Ruth, it was postmarked from Silver Springs, Florida;

and I knew this was the letter from James she had mentioned in her story.

"May I read it?"

"Of course! That's why I handed it to you." Careful to be as gentle as humanly possible, I pulled the letter out and unfolded it.

Dear Ruth,

I wish you could come visit me here. I think you would love it. There are walking paths around the springs, and there's a lucky palm called the horseshoe palm because it grows in an arch over the walkway! We have glass-bottom boats you can ride in, and see the fish. The water is so perfectly clear! Our village is small, but we function just like a Seminole village of our ancestors. We have craftsmen of all kinds, and the women prepare food and fetch water from the springs. I help my uncle make canoes. Guess what? A man from a movie studio in Hollywood came, and asked Uncle Charlie to make a canoe for a movie they would be filming right here at Silver Springs! Sure enough, a whole crew came in to set things up, and then the actors came. We got to meet Mr. Johnny Weismuller! He was very nice, and shook our hands, and posed for a picture with me and my uncle. He is going to keep the canoe when the movie is done. I know it's a Tarzan movie, but I'm not sure of the title. I will let you know if I can find out. If I get all my work done early, I'm allowed to go watch them film. As long as I'm quiet, that is. I sure do wish you were here. I'd show you all the sights, and introduce you to

Hollywood movie stars. Please write back, and tell me all about the things happening there.
Sincerely,
James

***

Ruth had to start packing for her trip home. I didn't like that she was leaving, and let her know it. She actually had to wipe a tear from her eye.

"I have a gift for you," I told her, handing her small envelope.

"What's this?"

"I couldn't decide what to give you since you really don't need anything else to haul home," I said, motioning towards all the boxes of keepsakes. "So, I made a donation in your honor to the new art therapy center for people with special needs. It seemed like your kind of charity."

She hugged me tightly. "That is the sweetest gift I've received in a long time," she said with a smile.

One last hug, and I walked out the door; hoping I'd see Ruth again in the near future, and hear more of her remarkable life story. I was in no mood to go to the office, so Bonnie took me to 9th Bar for espresso to cheer me up.

***

Once home, I pulled out my laptop and began working on an article about the case against the former police chief, specifically. This man was a study in narcissism. Even with witnesses and damning evidence, he acted as though he was too great an authority to be questioned, and sincerely expected it all to end with him receiving major apologies. I just shook my head, reading notes from the previous day's press conference. This guy was unreal.

It was near midnight when I emailed Katz my article. Five minutes later, he called me.

"This is good stuff! I mean, it's terrible what he's accused of doing, but your story—your info is really good. Finally, you're writing like you were meant to write!"

"Thanks, boss...I think."

"Any more problems with vandals?"

"No. So far that's the only incident."

"Good. But, if anything else does happen, give me a shout. I know a guy..."

"Uh huh. Right. Fortunately, I have a neighbor's dog who only barks at vandals—apparently. And, I have a baseball bat by the front door. I'm good."

"Seriously? My grandma has better security than that."

"Your grandma is dead."

"Yes, she is, and her cemetery has better security than your house!" Katz guffawed.

"You've had too much wine. Go to bed. Goodnight."

I hung up the phone, and grabbed a bottle of water from the fridge before heading to bed myself.

***

After an hour or so of sound slumber, I awoke to dog barking.

"You've got to be kidding me," I whispered to myself.

Fumbling around in the dark, I got dressed enough to not embarrass myself should neighbors see me standing outside; and took my baseball bat in my hands as I walked out the front door.
At first, I didn't notice anything unusual. I had parked my bike on the porch under the light. The front door was fine except for the crack from its previous stab wound. The dog kept barking.

I wandered down my driveway, looking in all direction; the baseball bat swung over my shoulder, ready to give someone a whack. Then, I notice a police car pulled over onto the side of the road about two houses down. Suddenly, I hear glass breaking behind me. Now the dog is really going nuts, barking incessantly. I run towards my house, and go inside. The kitchen and little dining area are in shambles; food tossed out of my fridge, chairs knocked over, my laptop smashed...and a window broken from the inside.

I heard tires squeal, and somehow knew it was the police car taking off—not to catch the perpetrator, but to get away from the crime scene. They had lured me out to leave me another message. Written on my refrigerator door in permanent marker were the words, "keep quiet."

***

I called Ben and left a message on his voicemail. He must've been asleep or he would've answered. Then, I called Katz, and told him everything that had just happened.

"You think it was the police?"

"I certainly don't think my seeing a police car parked in the darkest spot of the street was just a coincidence."

"No, I suppose not. We can change the article, if you want. Put a pseudonym on it, alter the wording…"

"No way! We are running that piece, and I'm going to the D.A.'s office first thing in the morning. Whatever I can do to stop these guys, I'm gonna do it."

"Whoa, you're suddenly eager to get more involved! I guess someone awakened the lion."

"Yes, someone did…the lion tamer's daughter."

***

That next morning, running on little sleep and more than the legal limit of coffee; I went to the district attorney, and told her of the witness intimidation going on.

"I'm not surprised," she admitted. "Somehow, these men still think they're above the law. Did you report the incident?"

"Only to Ben, uh...Lieutenant Maupin. He has a few men he trusts that he will notify."

"Very good. We hope to resolve this case soon, but with the money and connections these men have..."

"I know. But, if there's anything I can do to help solidify your case, please let me know. I'll help any way I can."

"That Ruth sure does have a way of motivating people."

"What makes you think she has something to do with this?"

"The only people who have made that kind of commitment to helping me put these men behind bars are people who have spoken with Ruth Cypress."

I chuckled. "Yes, well...she has certainly motivated me. And she didn't have to crack the whip."

✳✳✳

Over the next few months, it was (pardon the pun) a three-ring circus of hearings, testimonies, press conferences, and constant media attention. While it wasn't enjoyable, really; I did find myself more comfortable in the chaos than I had thought was even possible. There was a purpose. We were doing the right thing; standing up for others who needed us. What had once frightened me and forced me into a self-imposed prison of hiding and avoidance; now emboldened me, fueled me to write the next article, investigate further, tell what I knew. And, when it was all said and done, two criminal bigshots and four of their underlings went to prison.

***

Ben met me at 9th Bar for breakfast, and I convinced him to order the Bruce Lee.

"I can't believe how calm life feels now that the trials and sentencing are over with," Ben stated.

"Me either. I keep waiting for the next big thing to happen, but then I think—I don't want anything big to happen for a while."

Ben nodded in agreement. "At least not for a few more weeks! I have some vacation days coming up, and I plan on using them."

"Oh yeah? What'cha gonna do? Go fishing? Hit the theme parks?"

"Sleep. Maybe eat a little, but mostly…sleep."

"Yeah, a week's worth of sleep does sound pretty good," I confessed.

"When did we become such wusses?" Ben asked, laughing.

"Shut up and eat your Bruce Lee."

***

It had been a few weeks since my breakfast with Ben. I was in Katz' office discussing Ruth's story.

"You sure this is how you wanna go about it?" Katz asked, sitting behind his oversized desk, and peering at me over his reading glasses.

"Yeah, I'm sure. There's so much here, and it wouldn't feel right to leave stuff out."

"It's a very entertaining story. I think you're right about this. I'll call my publisher friend this afternoon. He loves reporters-turned-novelists. And with all the publicity you've gotten from this case, your book could really sell!"

"Whether it sells or not, I owe it to Ruth to publish her story."

"And you owe the whole experience to me, your boss—your friend."

"You gave me this assignment just to be a pain in the neck!"

Katz gave me an all knowing smirk. "Yeah, but so what? It worked out well in the end, didn't it?"

I shook my head. "It did. So, thank you, Katz for the opportunity, and thank you, Ruth, for the story of a lifetime."

"I'll drink to that," said Katz as he opened a desk drawer and pulled out a bottle of wine.

EPILOGUE

The following year, Ruth and I greeted each other once again; at an evening honoring the success of my first novel. People I didn't know, dressed in tuxedos and fancy dresses, offered their congratulations.

"Who are all these people?" I asked my literary agent, Scott.

"Fans, I guess? I don't even know. The publishing company invited a lot. But, forget all of them. There's just one person you really need to see."

Ruth walked up with her arms outstretched. "Michael, darling! I told you so!" were Ruth's first words, as she took my hands in hers.

"You told me so?"

"I said this time next year you'd be on the New York Times bestseller list, and well...here you are!"

"Predicting the future? You could finally have your own act!"

Ruth laughed. "I was never meant to perform."

"But, you were certainly meant to inspire. You're a star as far I'm concerned."

She hugged me and kissed my cheek.

"I have plans to visit your area again soon. Lizzie's house is going to be put up for sale, and I want to spend a few days to…reminisce."

"Give me the dates, and let's try to get together. I don't suppose you have any more stories for me."

"But, of course! Wait 'til you hear the story about my great-grandmother. She was the bearded lady!"

THE END

About The Author

Alyssa Helton lives in Florida with her husband, three children, and a large supply of coffee. For updates on newly published books and events, visit www.alyssahelton.com or like the "Alyssa Helton Author" Facebook page.

Look for these other books by Alyssa Helton:

Dogwood Alley

If the Crick Don't Rise (book 2 of the Dogwood Alley Series)

Joy In The Moring (book 3 of the Dogwood Alley Series)

And children's books (written as Nikki Helton, along with her husband Keith):

SamBoy Vs the Closet Monster

Bianfu the Bumblebee Bat

Coming Soon:
The Sugar King Short Stop (book 2 of the Michael Tallen Novel Series) Due fall of 2017

CPSIA information can be obtained
at www.ICGtesting.com
Printed in the USA
LVHW011556311221
707636LV00007B/244